ENGLISH FOR EVERYONE

學生英語語法全圖解

作者

本・弗蘭肯・道茲（Ben Ffrancon Dowds）是一位自由作家和文學翻譯家。他編寫的教科書和學習指南涵蓋多個學科，包括英語教學（ELT）、歷史和文學。他亦為兒童和成人撰寫一般性非小說類書籍。本曾於牛津大學修讀中世紀及現代語言學，並曾在法國和西班牙教授英語。他曾為《English for Everyone》系列多本書籍作出貢獻。

語言顧問

克里斯泰勒・韋克菲爾德（Christelle Wakefield）是一位教育顧問和編輯，專注於兒童英語教學（ELT）和現代外語領域。她曾在西班牙、墨西哥和瑞士任教，並從事教育出版工作超過 15 年，參與編寫全球各地學生及教師使用的課本及教材。

榮休教授蘇珊・巴爾杜恩（Professor Emerita Susan Barduhn）在英語教學（ELT）領域擁有豐富的國際經驗，曾擔任教師、培訓師、督導、經理、作者、導師、評核員、大會演講者和國際顧問等多種職務。她曾任國際英語教師協會（IATEFL）主席；奈洛比語言中心（The Language Center, Nairobi）主任兼聯合創始人；倫敦國際語言學校（International House, London）副總監；國際培訓學校（School for International Trainin）對外英語教學碩士課程（MATESOL）主席；現為英國文化協會（British Council）、傅爾布萊特計畫（Fulbright）、美國國務院（the U.S. State Department）、TransformELT 和 Consultants-e（TCE）的顧問。

ENGLISH
FOR EVERYONE
學生
英語語法全圖解

商務印書館

責任編輯 ： 陳朝暉　林加歡
裝幀設計 ： 趙穎珊
排　　版 ： 肖　霞
印　　務 ： 龍寶祺

Original Title: *English for Everyone Junior English Grammar: Makes Learning Fun and Easy*

本書中文繁體版由 DK 授權出版

學生英語語法全圖解

編　　著 ： 英國 DK 出版社
翻　　譯 ： 商務印書館編輯部
出　　版 ： 商務印書館（香港）有限公司
香港筲箕灣耀興道 3 號東滙廣場 8 樓
http://www.commercialpress.com.hk
發　　行 ： 香港聯合書刊物流有限公司
香港新界荃灣德士古道 220-248 號荃灣工業中心 16 樓
版　　次 ： 2025 年 7 月第 1 版第 1 次印刷

ISBN 978 962 07 6779 1
Published in Hong Kong

www.dk.com

Contents 目錄

1 Present simple 簡單現在式

參見：
簡單現在式否定句　第 2 單元
簡單現在式疑問句　第 3 單元

I play the guitar.

1.1 構成方法：規則動詞的簡單現在式

規則動詞遵循共同模式。構成規則動詞的簡單現在式要使用動詞基本形式。

當與 he 、 she 或 it 連用時，在動詞基本形式後面加 s 。

主語	動詞	句子其他部分
I	play	the guitar.

使用動詞基本形式。

提示！

我們使用動詞基本形式來構成英語中各種不同的句子。請參閱第 42 單元了解更多。

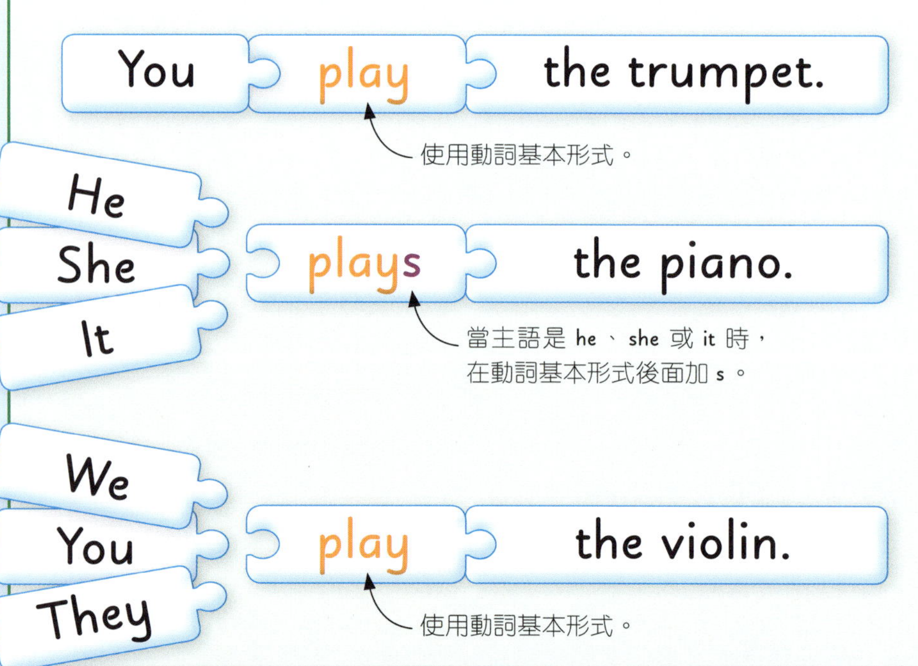

用法

使用簡單現在式談論事實、觀點或經常發生的事情。

1.2 拼寫規則：簡單現在式

大多數規則動詞的主語是 he 、 she 或 it 時，需在動詞基本形式後面加 s 。
但某些特定結尾的動詞，需加 es 而不是 s 。

play	watch	finish	go	miss	mix	buzz
↓	↓	↓	↓	↓	↓	↓
plays	watches	finishes	goes	misses	mixes	buzzes

更多例子

He **likes** cake.

She **watches** television in the evening.

They **live** in a pink house.

We **read** books every day.

The dog **loves** balls.

1.3 構成方法：「to be」簡單現在式

To be 在簡單現在式中是不規則動詞，變化形式與規則動詞不同。

用法

To be 簡單現在式用於表達事實、感受、情況和狀態。

更多例子

We **are** friends.

My dad **is** a teacher.

He **is** hot.

They **are** at the park.

You **are** sad.

1.4 簡單現在式：「to be」的縮略式

我們經常使用 am 、 is 和 are 的縮略式。

I am → I'm

You are → You're

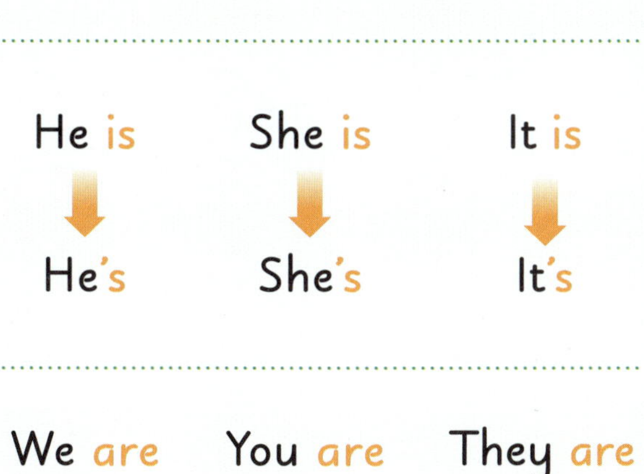

He is → He's

She is → She's

It is → It's

We are → We're

You are → You're

They are → They're

更多例子

I'm cold!

The cat's black.

It's dirty.

We're at school.

They're in the garden.

1.5 構成方法：「to have got」簡單現在式

To have got 是簡單現在式中的不規則動詞。
當主語為 he 、she 或 it 時，形式變成 has got 。

用法

使用 to have got 簡單現在式談論所擁有的物品、家庭成員和身體部位。

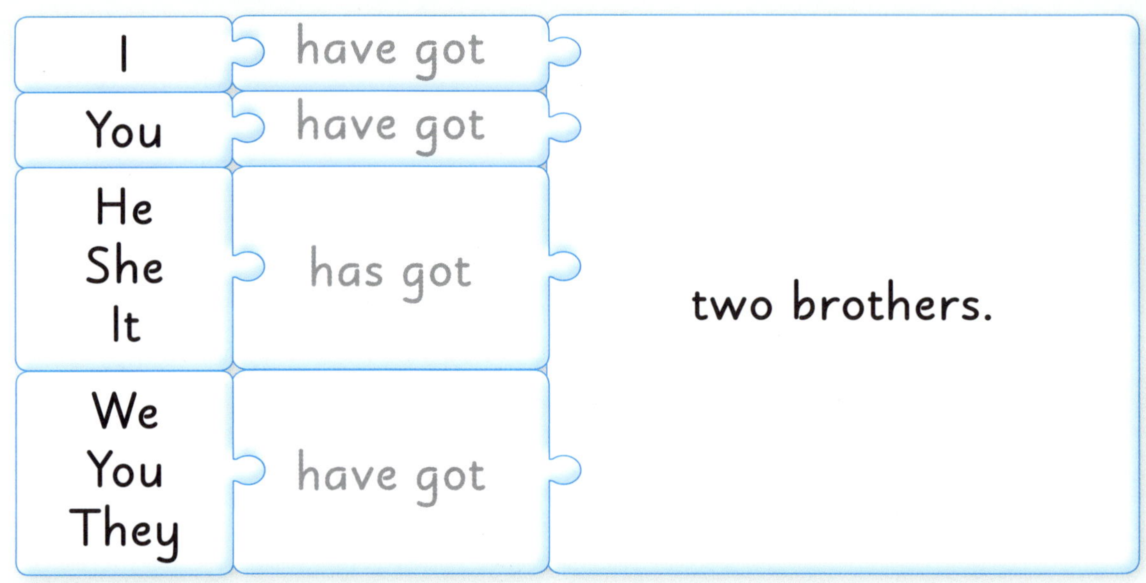

I	have got	two brothers.
You	have got	
He She It	has got	
We You They	have got	

I have got two brothers.

我們經常使用 have got 和 has got 的縮略式。

I have got → I've got
You have got → You've got

He has got → He's got
She has got → She's got
It has got → It's got

We have got → We've got
You have got → You've got
They have got → They've got

更多例子

I **have got** a new doll.

She **has got** two books.

You**'ve got** some lemonade.

They**'ve got** lots of pets.

He**'s got** a blue bag.

It**'s got** a ball.

We**'ve got** black hair.

Ben**'s got** a white rabbit.

2 Present simple negatives 簡單現在式否定句

參見：
簡單現在式　第 1 單元
簡單現在式疑問句　第 3 單元

I do not like milk.

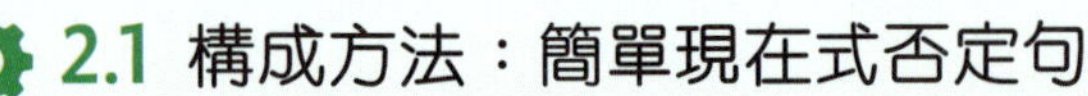

2.1 構成方法：簡單現在式否定句

大多數動詞的簡單現在式否定句，將 do not 或 does not 放在主要動詞基本形式前面。構成否定句時，不要在主要動詞後面加 s。

I like milk. → I do not like milk.

將 do not 放在主要動詞前面。

She likes milk. → She does not like milk.

不要在主要動詞後面加 s。

用法

使用簡單現在式否定句表達事實、觀點或不會發生的事情。

2.2 簡單現在式否定句：「do not」和「does not」的縮略式

我們經常將 do not 縮寫為 don't，
將 does not 縮寫為 doesn't。

這兩個詞連用時，字母 o 用撇號代替。

更多例子

I **do not enjoy** video games.

It **does not snow** in summer.

He **does not eat** meat.

Sara **doesn't wear** glasses.

They **don't live** in the city.

Tom **doesn't understand** the homework.

2.3 構成方法：「to be」簡單現在式否定句

構成 to be 簡單現在式否定句，只需在 am 、 is 或 are 後面加 not ，不需要使用 do not 或 does not 。

I am tired.

↓

I am not tired.

將 not 放在 am 、 is 或 are 後面。

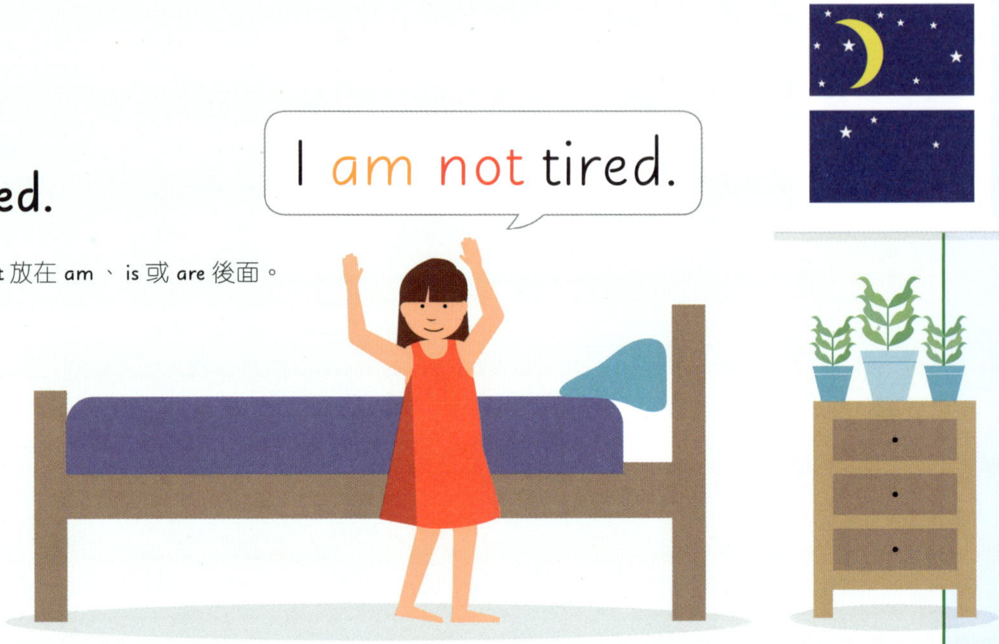

I am not tired.

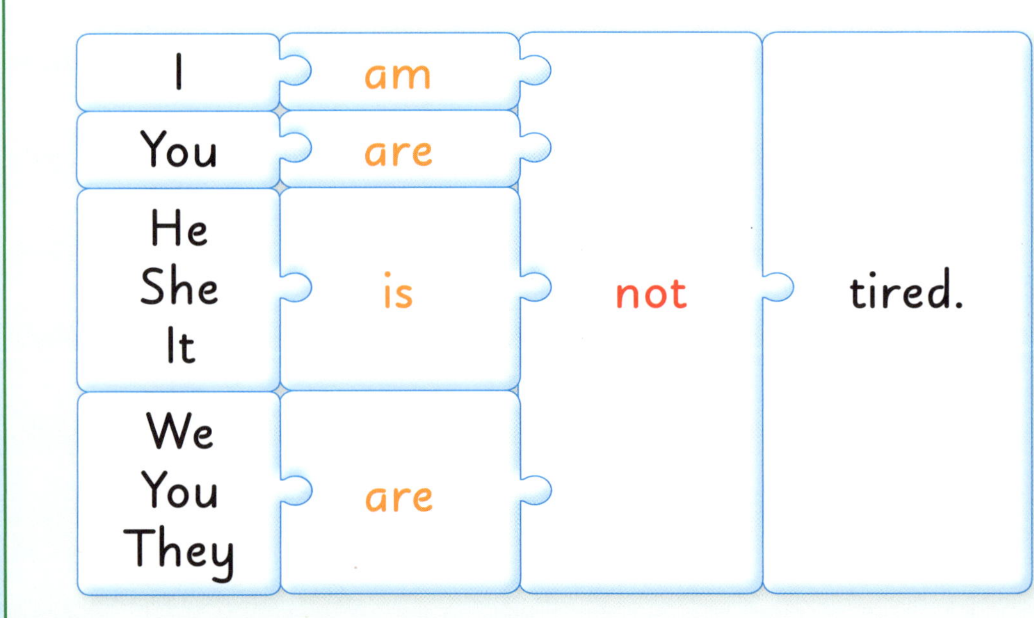

I	am	not	tired.
You	are		
He She It	is		
We You They	are		

用法

使用 to be 簡單現在式否定句表達事實、感受、情況或狀態。

2.4 簡單現在式否定句：「to be」的縮略式

除了 I am not 只有一種縮略式以外，其他 to be 簡單現在式否定句有兩種縮略式。

I am not

I'm not

You are not

You're not　You aren't

He is not

He's not　He isn't

She is not

She's not　She isn't

It is not

It's not　It isn't

We are not

We're not　We aren't

They are not

They're not　They aren't

更多例子

My coat **is not** red.

I **am not** seven,
I am eight.

He **is not** happy.

The robot**'s not** orange, it's blue.

Our house **isn't** big.

The dogs **aren't** dirty.

3 Present simple questions

簡單現在式疑問句

參見：
簡單現在式 第 1 單元
構成疑問句 第 38 單元

3.1 構成方法：簡單現在式疑問句

大多數動詞在簡單現在式開頭加上 do 或 does，就可以變成疑問句。
構成疑問句時，不要在主要動詞後面加 s。

You play tennis.

Do you play tennis?

在疑問句開頭加 Do。

在句尾加問號。

She plays tennis.

Does she play tennis?

在疑問句開頭加 Does。

不要在主要動詞後面加 s。

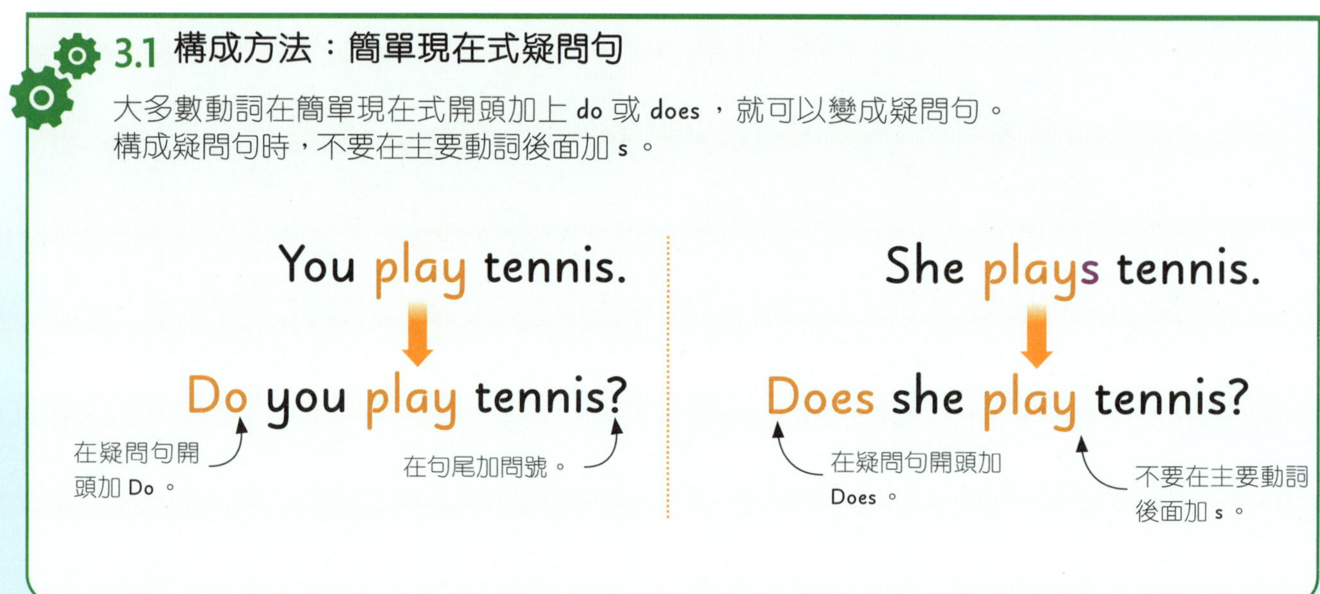

Do	I you	play	tennis?
Does	he she it	play	tennis?
Do	we you they	play	tennis?

用法

使用簡單現在式疑問句詢問事實、觀點或經常發生的事情。

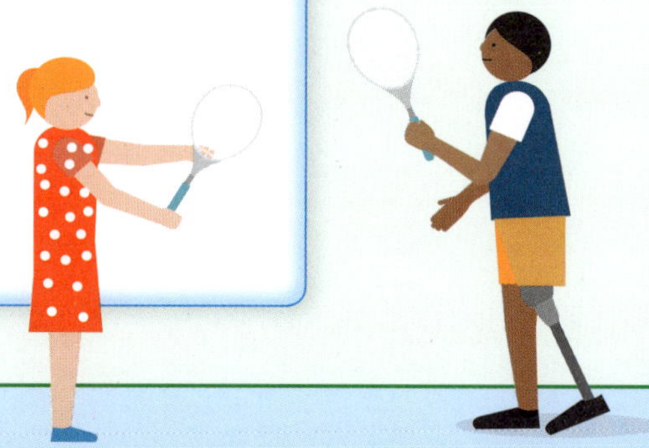

Do you play tennis?

Yes.

No.

更多例子

Do you want some cake?

Does she like baseball?

Do you speak English?

Does he play the guitar every day?

3.2 構成方法：「to be」簡單現在式疑問句

構成 to be 簡單現在式疑問句，需要將 am 、is 或 are 放在主語前面，不需要在句首加 do 或 does 。

You are excited.

這是使用 to be 簡單現在式的肯定句。

將 Are 放在主語 you 的前面。

Are you excited?

在句尾加上問號。

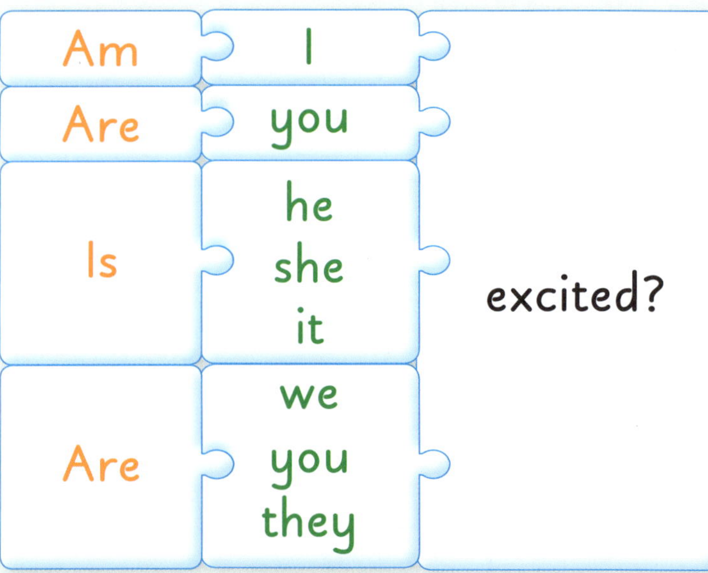

用法

使用 to be 簡單現在式疑問句詢問事實、感受、情況或狀態。

Are you excited?

Yes!

更多例子

Are you awake?

Is he a firefighter?

Is Jenny at home?

Is it cold outside?

Are they at the football match?

3.3 構成方法：「to have got」簡單現在式疑問句

構造 have got 或 has got 的簡單現在式疑問句，需將 have 或 has 放在主語前面，不需要在句首加 do 或 does 。

You have got a dog.

這是 to have got 簡單現在式肯定句。

Have you got a dog?

句尾加問號。

將 Have 放在主語 you 前面。

got 的位置保持不變。

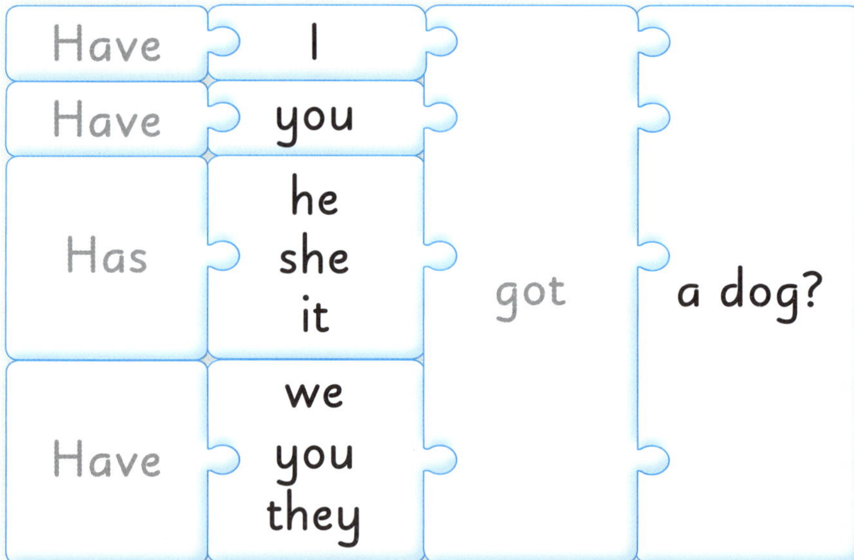

Have	I	got	a dog?
Have	you	got	a dog?
Has	he she it	got	a dog?
Have	we you they	got	a dog?

用法

使用 to have got 簡單現在式疑問句詢問所擁有的物品、家庭成員和身體部位。

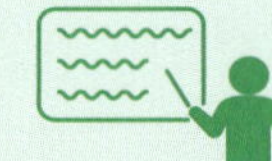

Have you got a dog?

更多例子

Has Kate got her hat?

Has he got a blue pencil?

Has she got a toothache?

Has Sara got a yellow bike?

Have you got any brothers?

4 Present continuous

現在進行式

參見：
簡單現在式 第 1 單元
不定式和基本形式 第 42 單元

I am running.

4.1 構成方法：現在進行式

構成現在進行式要在主語後面使用 am 、 is 或 are ，後面跟着主要動詞的現在分詞（participle）。

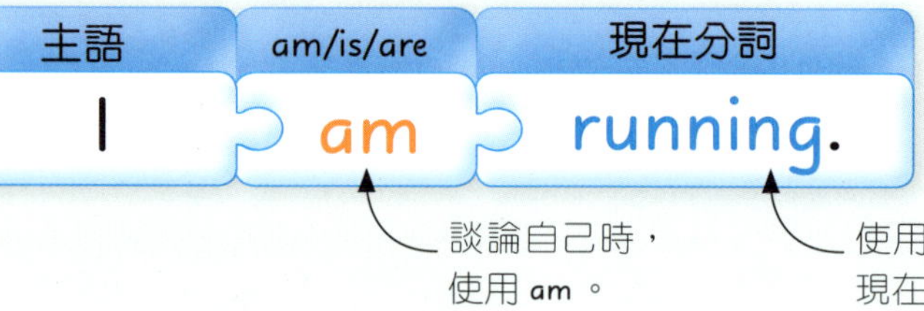

談論自己時，使用 am 。

使用主要動詞的現在分詞形式。現在分詞總是以 ing 結尾。

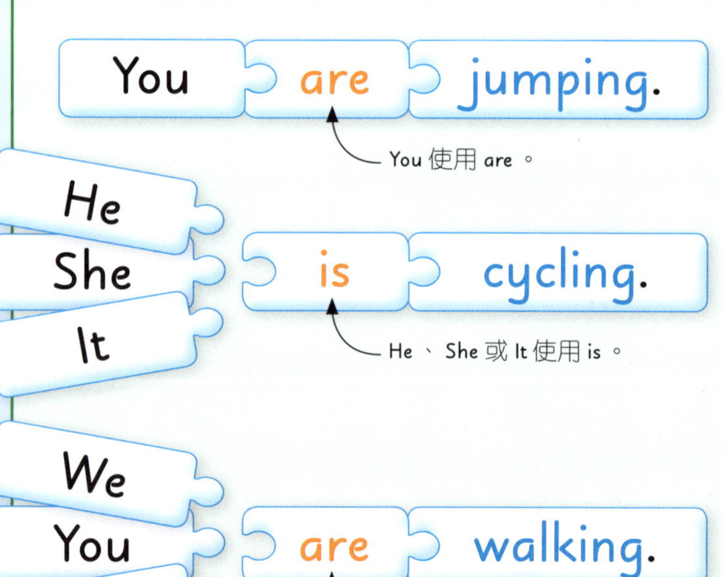

You 使用 are 。

He 、 She 或 It 使用 is 。

we, you 或 they 使用 are 。

用法

用現在進行式談論當前正在進行的動作。

4.2 拼寫規則：現在分詞

構成任何現在分詞，在基本形式後面加 ing 。
有時，基本形式在加 ing 前，拼寫會發生變化。

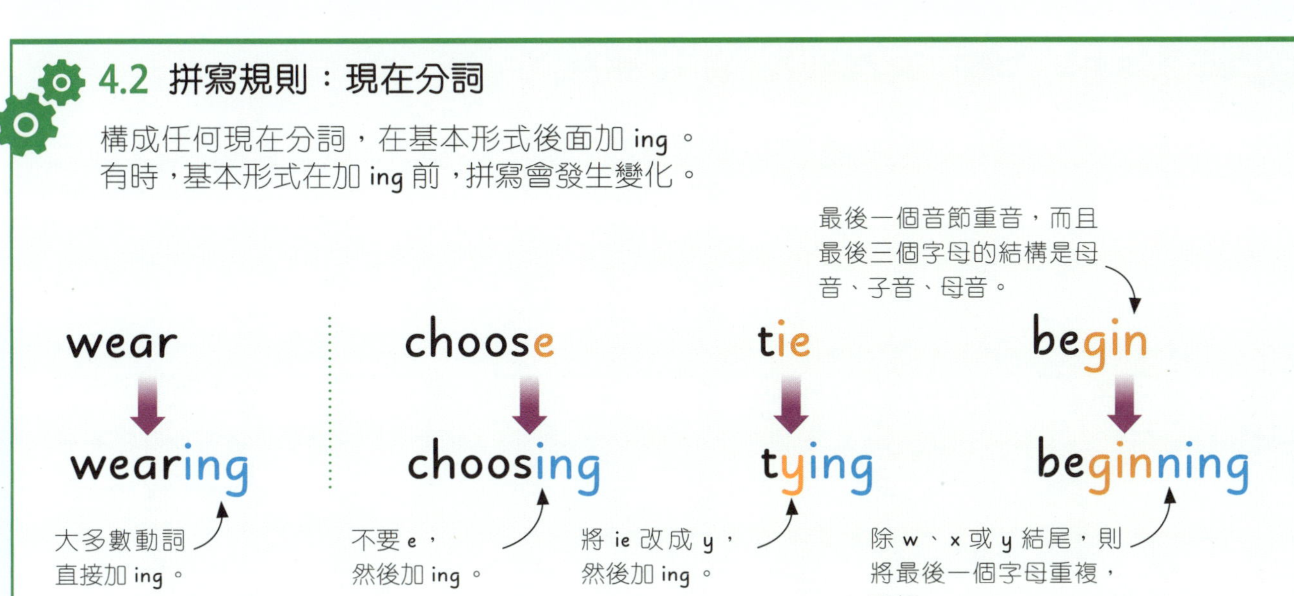

wear → **wearing**
大多數動詞直接加 ing 。

choose → **choosing**
不要 e ，然後加 ing 。

tie → **tying**
將 ie 改成 y ，然後加 ing 。

begin → **beginning**
最後一個音節重音，而且最後三個字母的結構是母音、子音、母音。
除 w 、 x 或 y 結尾，則將最後一個字母重複，再加 ing 。

更多例子

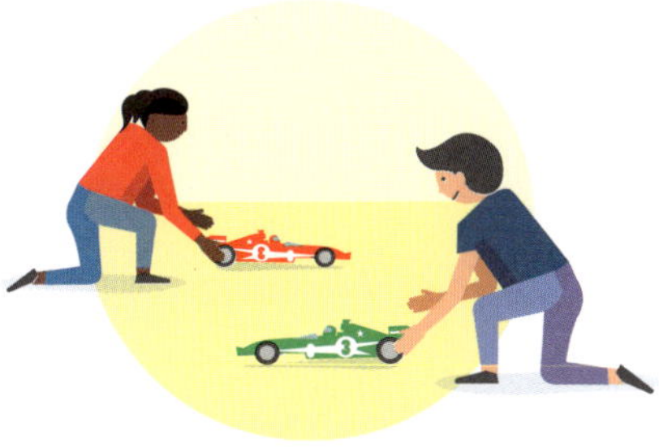

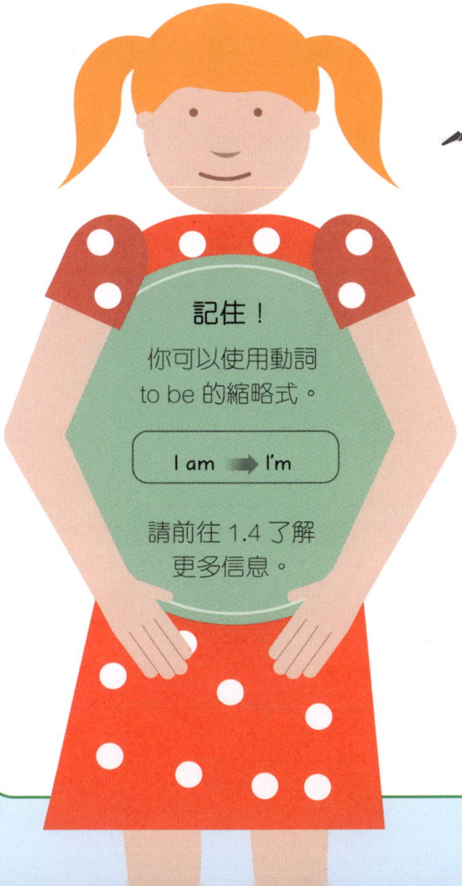

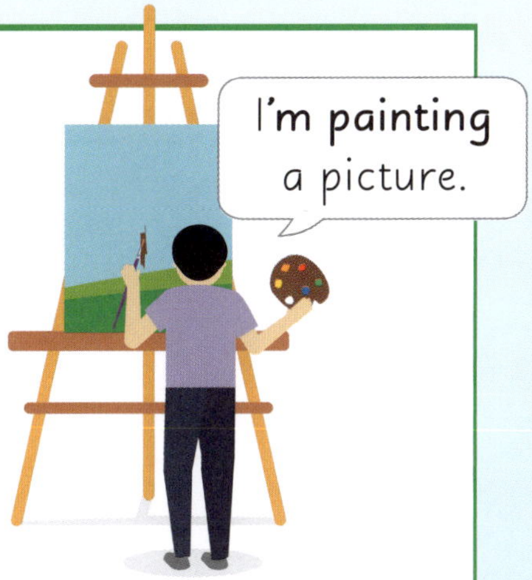

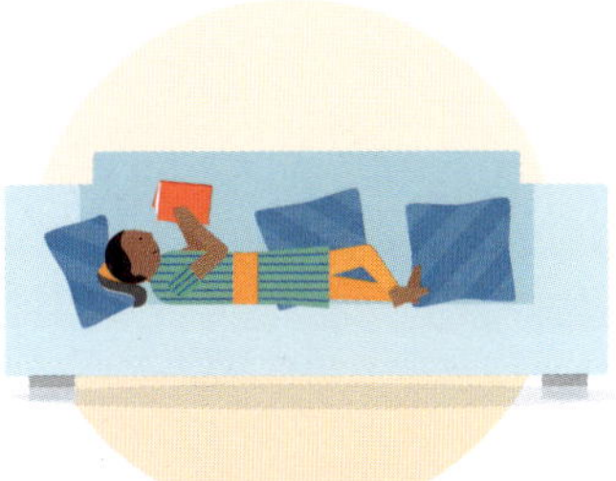

記住！
你可以使用動詞 to be 的縮略式。
I am → I'm
請前往 1.4 了解更多信息。

They **are playing**.

I'm painting a picture.

Sara **is lying** on the sofa.

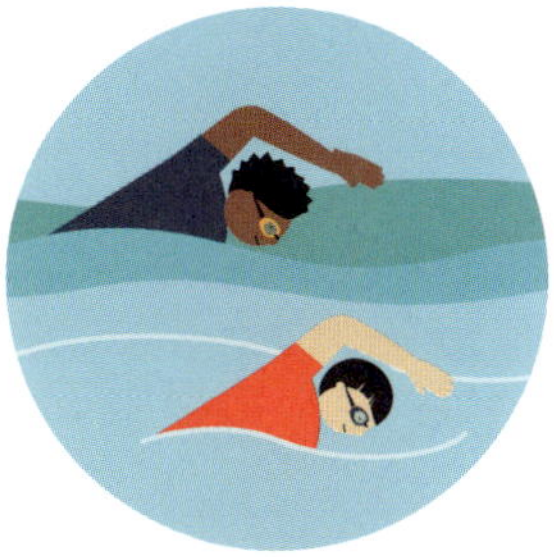

We**'re swimming** in the sea.

5 Present continuous negatives 現在進行式否定句

參見：
簡單現在式否定句　第 2 單元
現在進行式　第 4 單元

5.1 構成方法：現在進行式否定句

構成現在進行式否定句，將 not 放在 am、is 或 are 後面。

I am dancing.

I am not dancing.

將 not 放在 am、is 或 are 後面。

現在分詞保持不變。

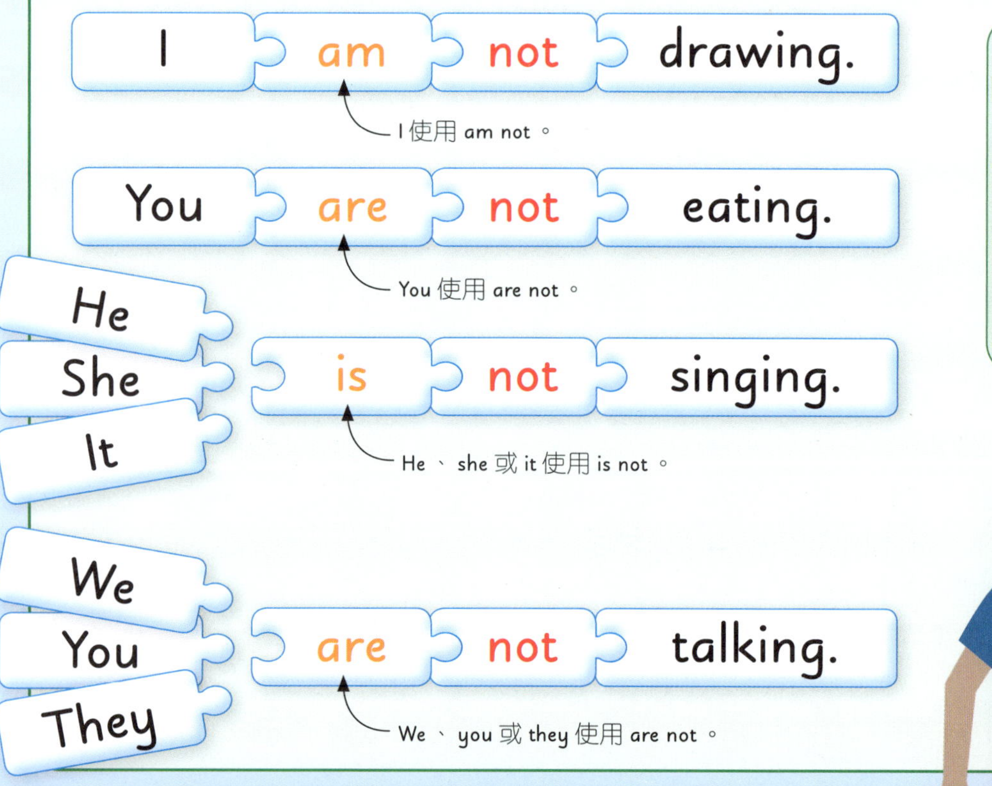

用法

現在進行式否定句用於表達目前這刻沒有發生的事情。

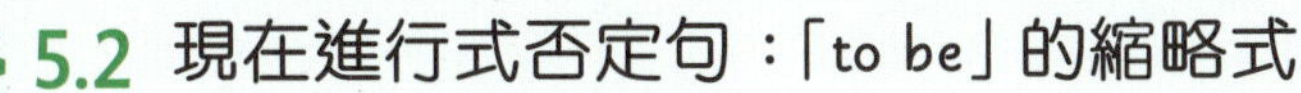

5.2 現在進行式否定句：「to be」的縮略式

除了 I am not 只有一種縮略式以外，
其他否定句有兩種縮略式。

I am not	You are not	He is not	She is not

I'm not	You're not	You aren't	He's not	He isn't	She's not	She isn't

It is not	We are not	They are not

It's not	It isn't	We're not	We aren't	They're not	They aren't

更多例子

It **is not** raining!

They **are not studying**,
they are playing.

She **isn't running**,
she's walking.

6 Present continuous questions 現在進行式疑問句

參見：
簡單現在式 第 1 單元
現在進行式 第 4 單元

Is it snowing?

6.1 構成方法：現在進行式疑問句

以現在進行式提問時，將 am 、 is 或 are 放在主語前面。

It is snowing.

將 is 放在主語 it 前面。

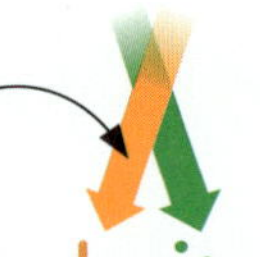

Is it snowing?

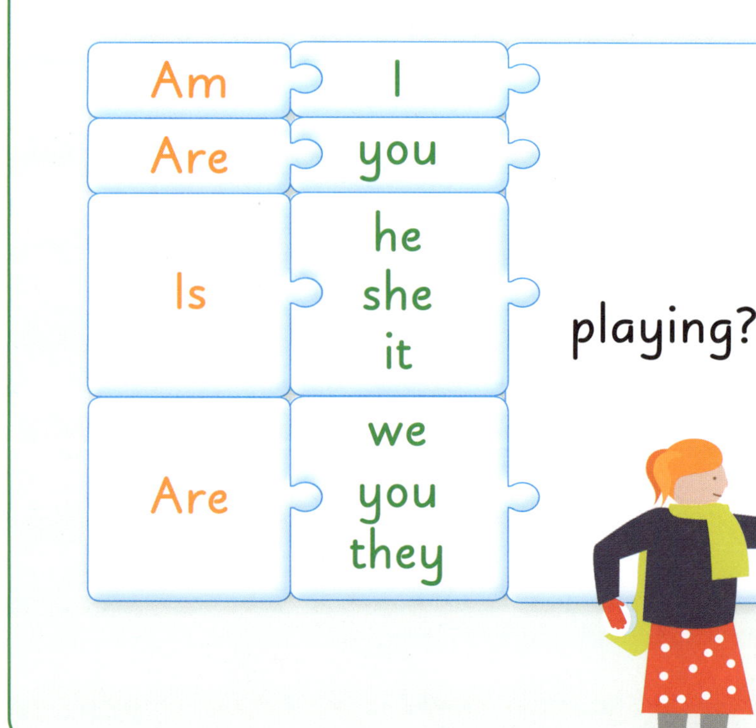

用法

用現在進行式疑問句詢問當前是否正發生事情。

更多例子

Are you learning English?

7 Present tenses overview 現在式概述

我們使用簡單現在式和現在進行式來談論現在的事情，
但它們應用於不同的情境中。

7.1 簡單現在式

構成規則動詞的簡單現在式，使用動詞基本形式。當主語是 he 、 she 或 it 時，在基本形式後面加 s 或 es 。更多內容請參閱第 1 單元。

Our car is blue.

這是事實。

I like video games.

這是意見。

Max reads a book every evening.

這是經常發生的事情。

用法

使用簡單現在式陳述事實或總是正確的事情。

使用簡單現在式用於表達意見。

使用簡單現在式描述習慣或經常發生的事情。

7.2 簡單現在式加「s」

在肯定句中，當主語為 he 、 she 或 it 時，總是在規則動詞後面加 s 或 es 。若句子是否定句或疑問句，即使主語是 he 、 she 或 it ，動詞後面也不會加 s 或 es 。

He starts school at 9 o'clock.

因為主語是 he ，而且是肯定句，所以加 s 。

He doesn't start school at 10 o'clock.

因為是否定句，所以不加 s 。

What time does he start school?

因為是疑問句，所以不加 s 。

7.3 現在進行式

構成現在進行式時，使用 am 、 is 或 are ，然後跟着現在分詞。更多內容請參閱第 4 單元。

I am painting a picture.

這是現在正在發生的事情。

It is snowing.

根據主語使用 am 、 is 或 are 。

They are riding their bikes.

使用主要動詞的現在分詞形式。

用法

使用現在進行式描述現在正在進行的動作。

7.4 比較簡單現在式和現在進行式

使用簡單現在式談論習慣或經常發生的事情。

We play table tennis on Mondays.

用現在進行式談論現在這刻正在進行的動作。

We are playing table tennis. It's fun!

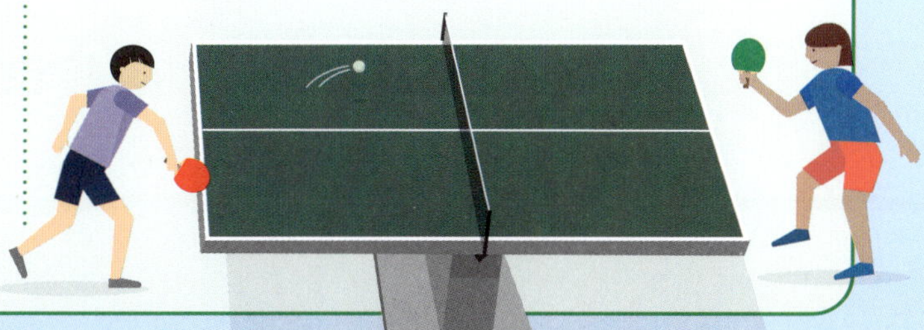

8 Past simple 簡單過去式

參見：
簡單過去式否定句　第 9 單元
簡單過去式疑問句　第 10 單元

I washed the car yesterday.

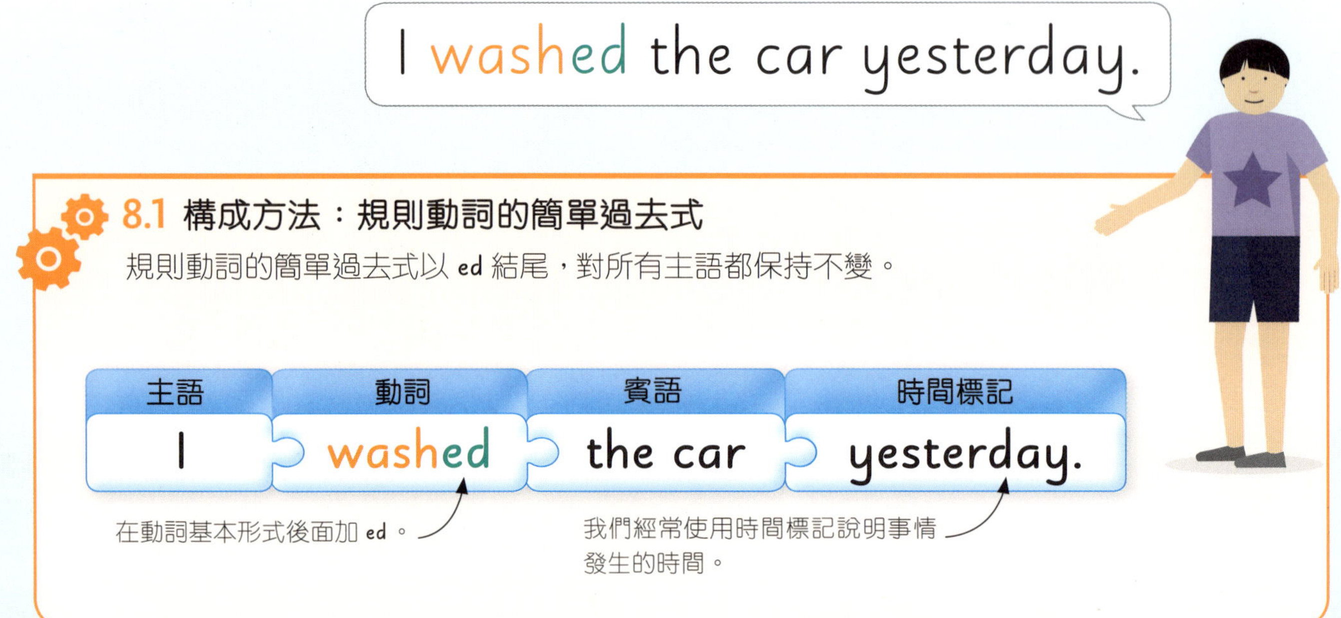

8.1 構成方法：規則動詞的簡單過去式

規則動詞的簡單過去式以 ed 結尾，對所有主語都保持不變。

主語	動詞	賓語	時間標記
I	washed	the car	yesterday.

在動詞基本形式後面加 ed。

我們經常使用時間標記說明事情發生的時間。

You	washed	the car.
He She It		
We You They		

這個動詞是簡單過去式。所有主語都使用相同形式。

用法

用簡單過去式談論在過去特定時刻發生的已完成動作。

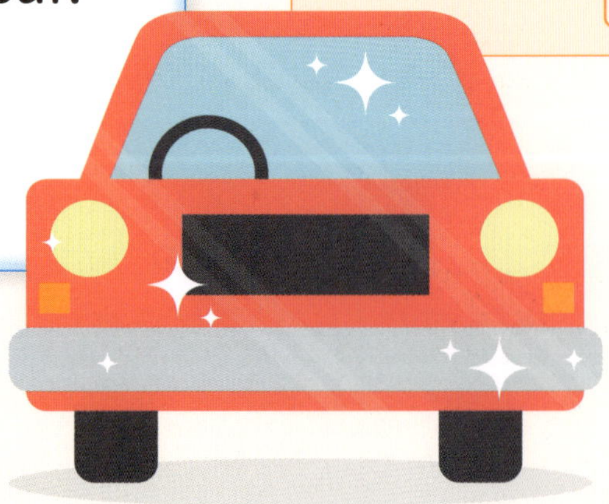

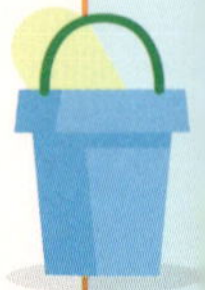

8.2 拼寫規則：簡單過去式

構成規則動詞的簡單過去式，需在動詞基本形式後面加 **ed**。
有時，基本形式在加 **ed** 前，拼寫會發生變化。

大多數動詞直接加 **ed**。

只加 **d**。

最後兩個字母的結構是子音和 **y**。

先將 **y** 改為 **i**，再加 **ed**。

最後兩個字母的結構是母音和子音。

將最後一個字母重複，再加 **ed**。

更多例子

I **cleaned** my bike yesterday.

The bus **stopped** in front of the school.

She **cried** because she **dropped** her toy.

We **danced** at the party last night.

They **planted** a tree last week.

8.3 簡單過去式中常見的不規則動詞

許多動詞在簡單過去式中是不規則的，有時看起來和基本形式相差很大。以下是過去式中一些最常見的不規則動詞。完整列表請參閱 R19 。

go	have	do	put	come	see
↓	↓	↓	↓	↓	↓
went	had	did	put	came	saw

8.4 構成方法：不規則動詞的簡單過去式

與規則動詞相同。除了 to be 以外，不規則動詞對所有主語都保持相同形式。

I You He She It We You They	went	to the shops yesterday.

We went to the shops yesterday.

8.5 構成方法：「to be」簡單過去式（past simple）

簡單過去式中，to be 有 was 和 were 兩種形式，是唯一會根據主語變化的動詞。

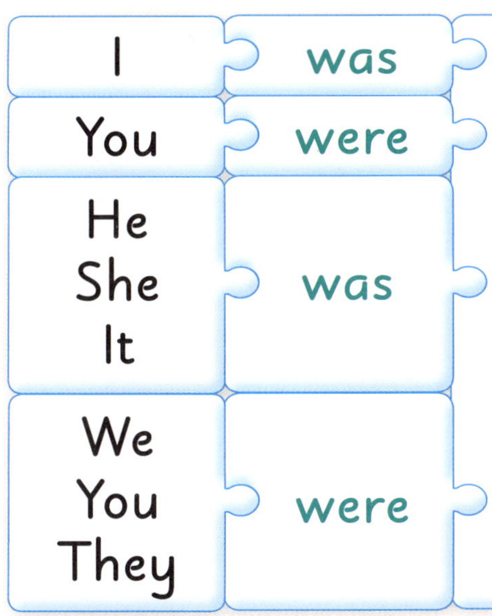

I	was	at the beach last week.
You	were	
He She It	was	
We You They	were	

用法

用 to be 簡單過去式談論過去的事實、感受、情況或狀態。

更多例子

Ben **came** to my house last week.

We **had** pasta for dinner last night.

They **were** very tired after school.

9 Past simple negatives
簡單過去式否定句

參見：
簡單過去式　第 8 單元
不定式和基本形式　第 42 單元

I did not like the cake.

9.1 構成方法：簡單過去式否定句

構成簡單過去式否定句，需在主要動詞前面加 did not，而且對所有主語都保持不變。主要動詞始終保持基本形式，不要使用簡單過去式形式或加 s。

I liked the cake.

I did not like the cake.

在主要動詞前面加 did not。

主要動詞保持基本形式。

I You He She It We You They	did not	like	the cake.

用法

用簡單過去式否定句談論過去未發生的動作或狀態。

9.2 簡單過去式否定句：「did not」的縮略式

我們經常將 did not 縮寫為 didn't。

I did not like the cake.

I didn't like the cake.

Did 和 not 連用時，字母 o 用撇號代替。

更多例子

He **didn't wear** a hat at the party.

We **did not play** in the park yesterday.

They **did not understand** the test.

Andy **didn't drink** his juice.

9.3 構成方法：「to be」簡單過去式否定句

構成 to be 簡單過去式否定句，需要在 was 或 were 後面加 not，不需要使用 did not 或 didn't。

It **was** warm.

It **was** **not** warm.

在 was 或 were 後面加 not。

It was not warm yesterday.

I	was	not	warm.
You	were		
He She It	was		
We You They	were		

用法

使用 to be 簡單過去式否定句談論過去的事實、情況或狀態。

更多例子

The dog **was not** hungry.

The shop **was not** open.

The balls **were not** red.

9.4 簡單過去式否定句：「was not」和「were not」的縮略式

我們經常將 was not 縮寫為 wasn't ， were not 縮寫為 weren't 。

were not

was 和 not 連用時，字母 o 用撇號代替。

were 和 not 連用時，字母 o 用撇號代替。

更多例子

I **wasn't** very well last week.

The film **wasn't** interesting.

The questions **weren't** too difficult.

The boots **weren't** clean.

It **wasn't** cold this morning.

The cat **wasn't** white, it was black.

10 Past simple questions
簡單過去式疑問句

參見：
簡單過去式　第 8 單元
構成疑問句　第 38 單元

Did you watch the game?

10.1 構成方法：簡單過去式疑問句

構成簡單過去式疑問句，需要在主語前面加 did，以及主要動詞使用基本形式，不要使用過去式，也不要加 s。 Did 適用於所有主語。

You watched the game.

Did you watch the game?

將 Did 放在疑問句開頭。

主要動詞保持基本形式。

在句尾加問號。

Did	I you he she it we you they	watch the game?

用法

用簡單過去式疑問句詢問過去已完成的動作。

更多例子

Did they catch a fish?

Did she finish the race?

Did you wear a red dress to the party?

Did Jess play football today?

Did it rain yesterday?

Did he see a horse at the farm?

Did you go camping last summer?

Did you buy a new hat?

10.2 構成方法：「to be」簡單過去式疑問句

構成 to be 簡單過去式疑問句，需要在主語前面加 was 或 were ，不需要使用 did 。

You were at the party yesterday.

Were you at the party yesterday?

在主語 you 前面加 Were 。　　在句尾加問號。

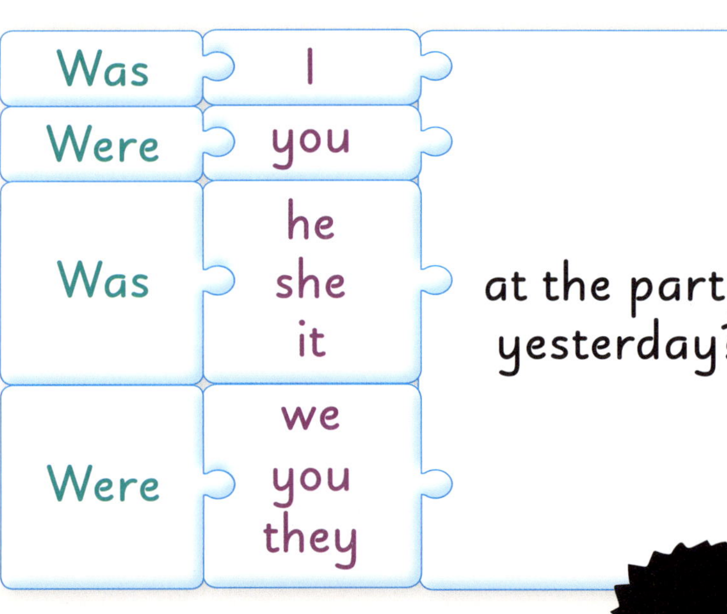

Was	I	at the party yesterday?
Were	you	
Was	he she it	
Were	we you they	

用法

用 to be 簡單過去式疑問句詢問過去的事實、情況和狀態。

Were you at the party yesterday?

Yes.

更多例子

Was I fast?

Were you at the park yesterday?

Was the slide big?

Was the clown funny?

Was she excited to see you?

Was school fun today?

Were you scared on the rollercoaster?

Were Dad and Sofia happy to visit Grandma?

11 Past continuous
過去進行式

參見：
現在進行式 第 4 單元
簡單過去式 第 8 單元

11.1 構成方法：過去進行式

構成過去進行式時，使用 was 或 were，然後跟着現在分詞。

主語	was/were	現在分詞	句子其他部分
The sun	was	shining	in the sky.

根據主語使用 was 或 were。

主要動詞使用現在分詞形式。

11.2 過去進行式的用法

過去進行式有兩種用法。

用法

過去進行式用於講述故事。

過去進行式

The birds were singing in the trees. It was a beautiful day.

過去進行式用於談論過去正在進行的動作，被另一個動作打斷的情況。

過去進行式

I was sleeping when an apple fell on my head.

用簡單過去式表示打斷的動作。

更多例子

The boys **were running** through the forest.

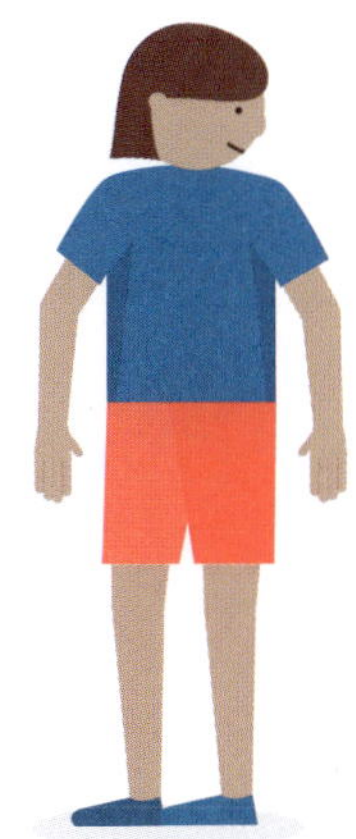

I **was playing** basketball when you called yesterday.

The girls **were having** fun together.

The ducks **were swimming** in the water.

Maria **was listening** to music when Andy arrived.

記住！

大部分現在分詞在基本形式後面加 ing。有些現在分詞有不同的拼寫規則。詳情請參閱 4.2。

It was a cold day. Snow **was falling**.

I **was playing** in the garden when it started to rain.

12 Past continuous negatives
過去進行式否定句

參見：
簡單過去式否定句 第 9 單元
過去進行式 第 11 單元

12.1 構成方法：過去進行式否定句

構成過去進行式否定句，在 was 或 were 後面加 not。

The children were drawing.

The children were not drawing.

在 was 或 were 後面加 not。

現在分詞保持不變。

12.2 過去進行式否定句的用法

過去進行式否定句有兩種用法。

用法

用過去進行式否定句講述故事。

Sara was not listening to music. She was reading a book.

用過去進行式否定句談論過去某個動作發生時，另一個動作並未進行的情況。

I was not paying attention when I fell over the blocks.

用簡單過去式表示打斷性動作。

12.3 過去進行式否定句：「was not」和「were not」的縮略式

我們經常將 was not 縮寫為 wasn't，were not 縮寫為 weren't。

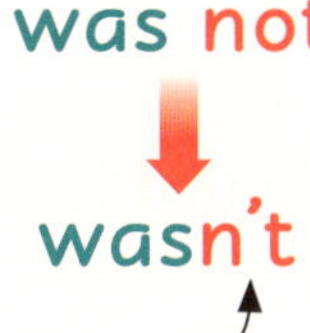

Was 和 not 連用時，字母 o 用撇號代替。

Were 和 not 連用時，字母 o 用撇號代替。

更多例子

The computer **wasn't working.**

It **wasn't raining** when we arrived at the park.

We **were not walking,** we were riding our bikes.

記住！

大部分現在分詞是在基本形式後面加 ing。有些現在分詞有不同的拼寫規則。詳情請參閱 4.2。

They **weren't surfing,** they were sailing!

Sofia's mum took a photo, but Sofia **wasn't smiling.**

13 Past continuous questions 過去進行式疑問句

參見：
過去進行式 第 11 單元
疑問詞 第 40 單元

Were you playing in your room?

Yes.

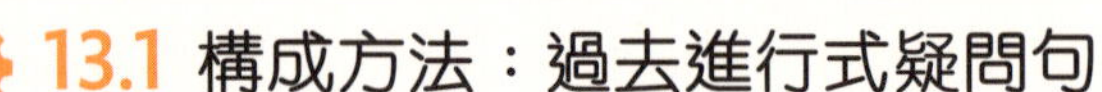

13.1 構成方法：過去進行式疑問句

構成過去進行式疑問句，將 was 或 were 放在主語前面。

You were playing in your room.

將 were 放在主語 you 前面。

Were you playing in your room?

現在分詞的位置保持不變。

在句尾加問號。

Was	I	reading?
Were	you	
Was	he she it	
Were	we you they	

用法

用過去進行式疑問句詢問過去正在進行的動作。

更多例子

Were you skipping this morning?

What **was Ben studying** in the library at lunchtime?

Was it snowing at the park?

Was he playing tennis when you saw him?

What **was Dad cooking** when you got home?

What **were you buying** at the shop yesterday?

Why **were they whispering**?

Where **was Sara going** yesterday morning?

記住！

大部分現在分詞是在基本形式後面加 ing。有些現在分詞有不同的拼寫規則。請參閱 4.2 了解更多。

14 Present perfect
現在完成式

參見：
時間介詞　第 74 單元
不規則動詞　第 R19 小節

I have finished dinner.

14.1 構成方法：現在完成式

構成現在完成式，在 have 或 has 後面使用過去分詞（participle）。

主語	have/has	過去分詞	句子其他部分
I	have	finished	dinner.

使用 have 或 has 構成現在完成式。

構成規則動詞的過去分詞，在動詞基本形式後面加 ed。

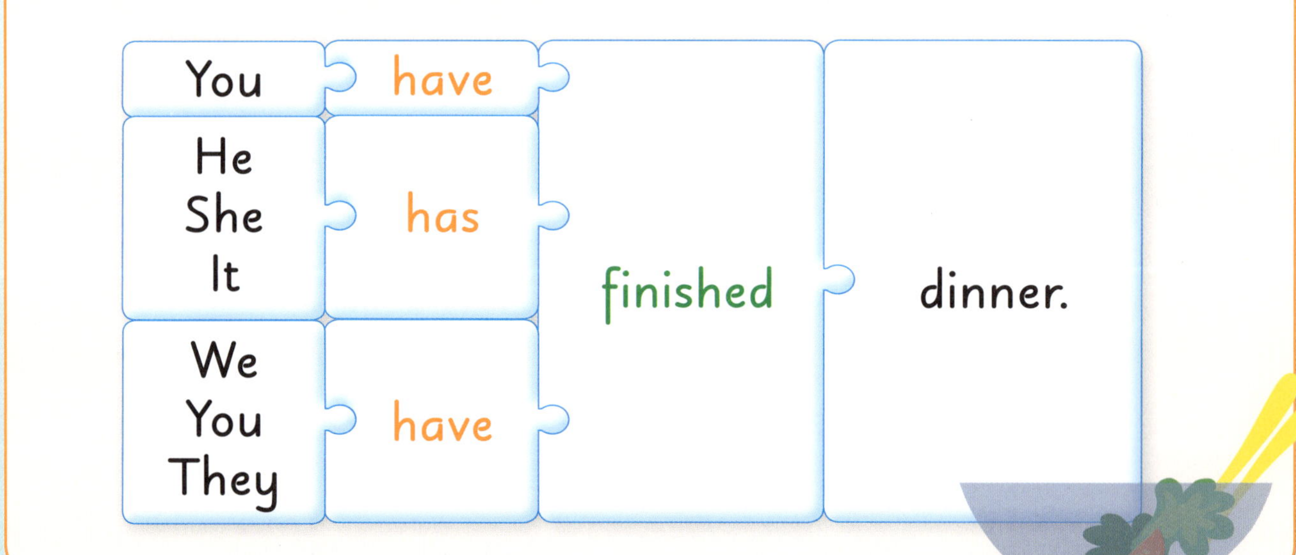

You	have	finished	dinner.
He She It	has		
We You They	have		

14.2 現在完成式的用法

現在完成式有五種用法。

	用法
 I have finished lunch.	用這個時態傳遞消息或談論沒有具體時間的近期事件。
 I have visited the museum five times.	用這個時態談論過去重複發生的動作。
 Oh no! I have dropped my keys!	用這個時態談論與現在有關係的過去動作或狀態。
 I have painted three pictures this morning.	用這個時態談論在一段仍未結束的時間內發生的動作。
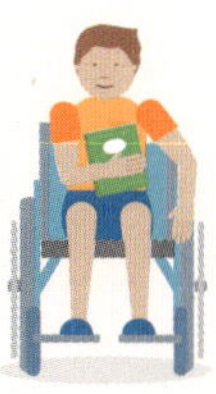 I have studied English for two years.	用這個時態談論從過去開始，持續到現在，並可能持續到未來的動作或狀態。

我們經常將 for 和 since 與現在完成式連用。

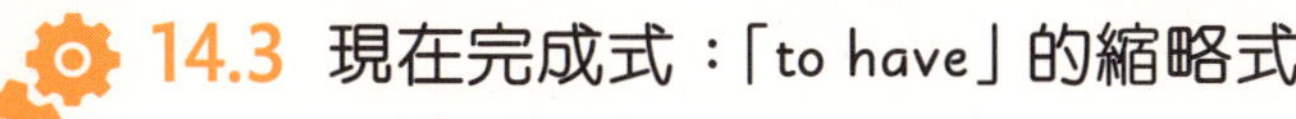

14.3 現在完成式：「to have」的縮略式

我們經常使用 have 和 has 的縮略式。

I have	You have	He has	She has	It has	We have	You have	They have

I've	You've	He's	She's	It's	We've	You've	They've

14.4 拼寫規則：規則動詞的過去分詞

構成規則動詞的過去分詞，在基本形式後面加 **ed**。
有時加 **ed** 前，基本形式的拼寫會發生變化。

大多數動詞直接加 **ed**。

只加 **d**。

最後兩個字母的結構是子音和 **y**。

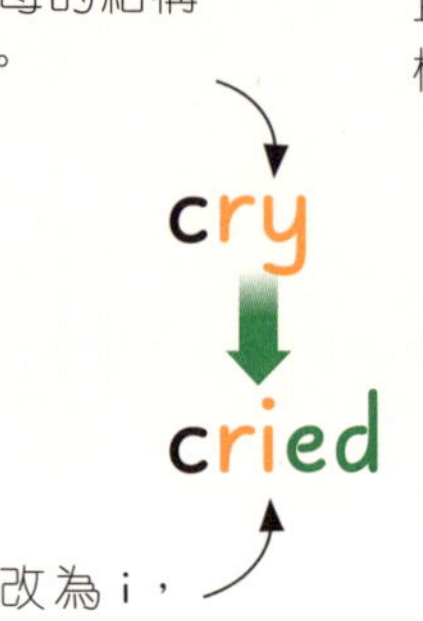

將 **y** 改為 **i**，再加 **ed**。

最後一個音節是重音，且最後三個字母的結構是子音、母音、子音。

最後一個字母重複，然後加 **ed**。

更多例子

She's **lived** in this house since 1975.

We've **arrived** in New York.

I've **watched** two films this evening.

Claire **has joined** the football team.

I **have invited** my friends to my party.

14.5 不規則動詞的過去分詞

英語動詞有許多不規則過去分詞，不以 ed 結尾。
以下是一些最常見的不規則過去分詞，更多列表，請參見 R19。

go	be	have	do	come	see
↓	↓	↓	↓	↓	↓
gone	been	had	done	come	seen

14.6「Gone」和「been」

Gone 是 to go 的過去分詞， been 是 to be 的過去分詞。
我們用這兩個詞來談論去某個地方，但兩者的意思不同。

Sara has gone to Spain.

這表示 Sara 去了西班牙，現在仍在西班牙。

Sara has been to Spain.

這表示 Sara 去過西班牙，但她已經回來了。

更多例子

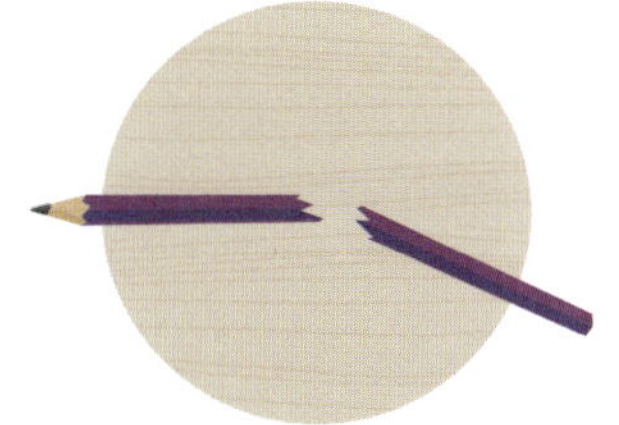

Look! You've **broken** your pencil!

Oh no! Andy **has forgotten** his book.

Maria is sad. She **has lost** her doll.

15 Present perfect negatives

現在完成式否定句

參見：
時間副詞 第 69 單元
時間介詞 第 74 單元

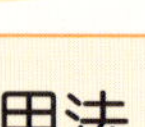

15.1 構成方法：現在完成式否定句

構成現在完成式否定句時，在 have 或 has 與過去分詞之間加 not。

I **have** been to the beach this year.

I **have not** been to the beach this year.

將 not 放在 have 或 has 後面。

Been 是 to be 的過去分詞形式。

用法

了解現在完成式的具體用法，請參閱第 14 單元。

15.2 現在完成式否定句：「have not」和「has not」的縮略式

我們經常將 have not 縮寫為 haven't，將 has not 縮寫為 hasn't。

have not → haven't

has not → hasn't

have 和 not 連用時，字母 o 用撇號代替。

has 和 not 連用時，字母 o 用撇號代替。

更多例子

I **have not eaten** my breakfast yet.

We **haven't watched** television today.

She **hasn't flown** on a plane before.

16 Present perfect questions
現在完成式疑問句

參見：
時間副詞 第 69 單元
時間介詞 第 74 單元

16.1 構成方法：現在完成式疑問句

使用現在完成式提問，需將 have 或 has 放在主語前面。

You have been on a rollercoaster.

Have you been on a rollercoaster?

把 Have 放在主語 you 前面。

用法

了解何時使用現在完成式，請參閱第 14 單元。

更多例子

Have you read this book?

Has it snowed today?

Have they finished their pictures yet?

Have you seen my teddy bear?

Have you studied English this week?

17 Past tenses overview 過去式概述

我們使用簡單過去式、現在完成式和過去進行式描述過去的事件，但三者使用情況不同。

17.1 簡單過去式

構成大部分規則動詞的簡單過去式，需在動詞基本形式後面加 ed。更多內容請參閱第 8 單元。

這是過去已完成的動作。

We baked ten biscuits yesterday.

用法

簡單過去式用於談論在過去某個已結束時段中發生的已完成動作。

17.2 現在完成式

構成現在完成式，使用 have 或 has，然後跟着過去分詞。更多內容請參閱第 14 單元。

這個動作是發生在仍未結束的時段中。

We have eaten three biscuits today.

用法

現在完成式用於談論在尚未結束的時段中發生的動作。

17.3 比較簡單過去式與現在完成式

We baked ten biscuits yesterday.

We have eaten three biscuits today.

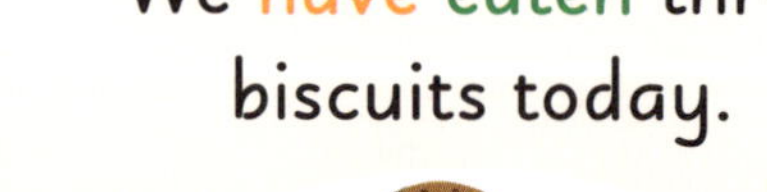

昨天

今天

這是在現已結束的一段時間內發生的。

這發生在仍未結束的時段內。他們今天可能會吃更多餅乾。

17.4 過去進行式

構成過去進行式使用 was 或 were，後面跟着現在分詞。更多內容請參閱第 11 單元。

It was a windy day and leaves were falling from the trees.

這是在講述一個關於過去的故事。

At 6 o'clock last night, we were watching television.

這是過去一個持續的動作。

用法

過去進行式用於講述一個故事。

用法

過去進行式用於談論過去一個持續的動作。

17.5 簡單過去式和過去進行式的結合使用

We were having dinner when the phone rang.

過去

現在

簡單過去式的動作打斷了過去進行式的動作。

18「Going to」

參見：
簡單現在式 第 1 單元
將來式概述 第 25 單元

18.1 構成方法：「going to」

用 going to 造句時，使用 am、is 或 are，後面跟着 going to，再加主要動詞的基本形式。

主語	am/is/are	going to	基本形式	句子其他部分
Sofia	is	going to	win	the race!

根據主語使用 am、is 或 are。

Going to 總是保持不變。

當主語為 he、she 或 it 時，基本形式不加 s。

18.2「going to」的用法

going to 有兩種用法。

用法	
Going to 用於根據現有證據對未來作出預測，或當你知道事情將會發生時。	She is going to catch the ball.
Going to 用於談論你在現在這個時刻之前，已經制定了的計劃或決定。	I am going to ride my bike to school tomorrow.

更多例子

He **is going to score**.

I'**m going to read** my book later.

They **are going to grow** some flowers.

Oh no! Max **is going to fall over**.

We'**re going to play** video games after school.

We **are going to paint** some pictures.

注意事項！

你可以使用 **to be** 的縮略式。

I am → I'm

更多內容請參閱 1.4。

Careful! You'**re going to drop** the drinks!

Look at the clouds! It'**s going to rain** soon.

19 "Going to" negatives
「Going to」否定句

參見：
簡單現在式否定句 第 2 單元
「Going to」 第 18 單元

19.1 構成方法：「Going to」否定句

用 going to 構成否定句時，在 going to 前面加 not 。

We are going to arrive on time.

We are not going to arrive on time.

在 going to 前面加 not 。

用法

了解何時使用包括 going to 的句子，請參閱第 18 單元。

更多例子

It is not going to snow tomorrow.

He isn't going to play video games today.

They're not going to find me!

注意！

is not 和 are not 有兩種縮寫方式，詳情請參閱 2.4 。

20 "Going to" questions
「Going to」疑問句

參見：
簡單現在式疑問句 第 3 單元
「Going to」 第 18 單元

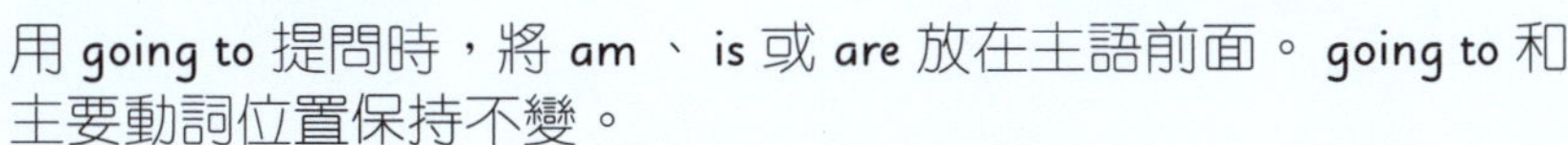

20.1 構成方法：
Going to 疑問句

用 going to 提問時，將 am 、 is 或 are 放在主語前面。 going to 和主要動詞位置保持不變。

They are going to be late.

Are they going to be late?

將 Are 放在主語 they 前面。

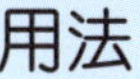

用法

了解何時使用 going to 的句子，請參閱第 18 單元。

更多例子

Are you going to drink your juice?

Are we going to go to the beach today?

It's very cloudy outside. Is it going to rain soon?

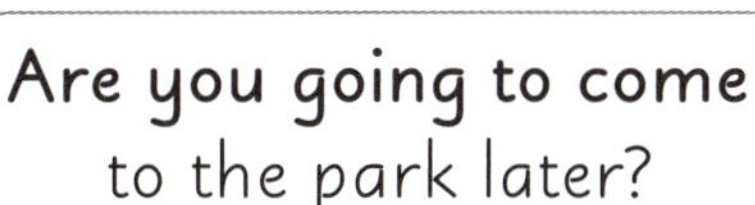

Is she going to sing a song?

21 「Will」

參見：
「Going to」 第 18 單元
將來式概述　第 25 單元

21.1 構成方法：「Will」

構成 will 句子時，will 後面跟着主要動詞基本形式。
will 對所有主語都保持不變。

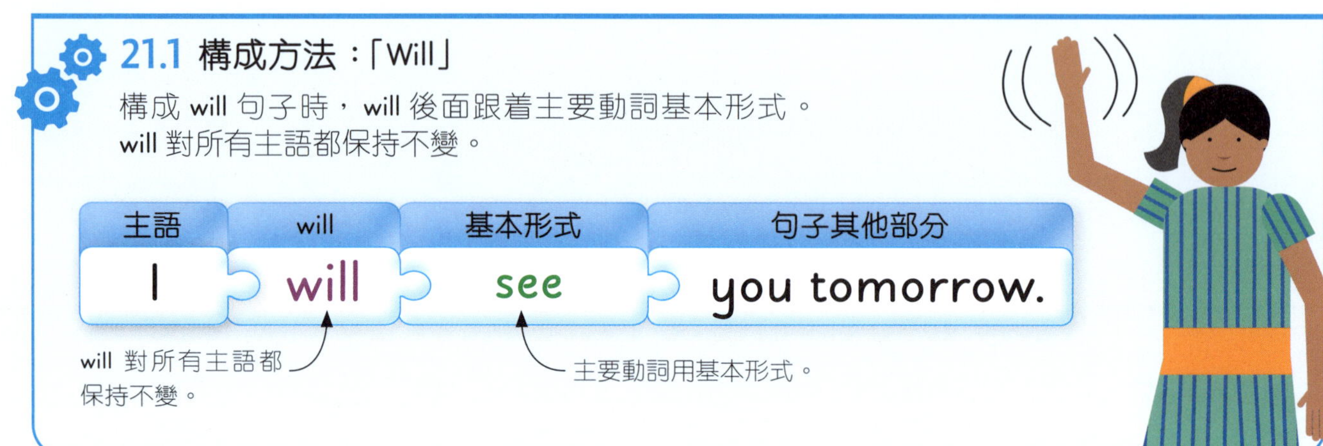

21.2 「will」的用法

will 有四種用法。

用法	
使用 will 談論你剛才做出的決定。	I will have a glass of milk.
使用 will 作出承諾。	I will call you when I get home.
使用 will 作出在當下沒有任何證據的預測。	I think you will love this book.
使用 will 主動提出做某件事情。	I will help you with those bags.

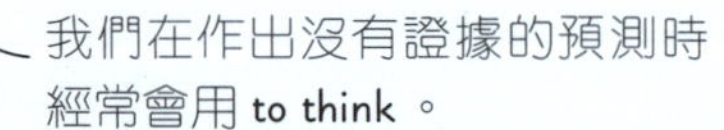
我們在作出沒有證據的預測時，經常會用 to think。

21.3 「Will」：縮略式

我們經常將 will 縮寫為 'll。

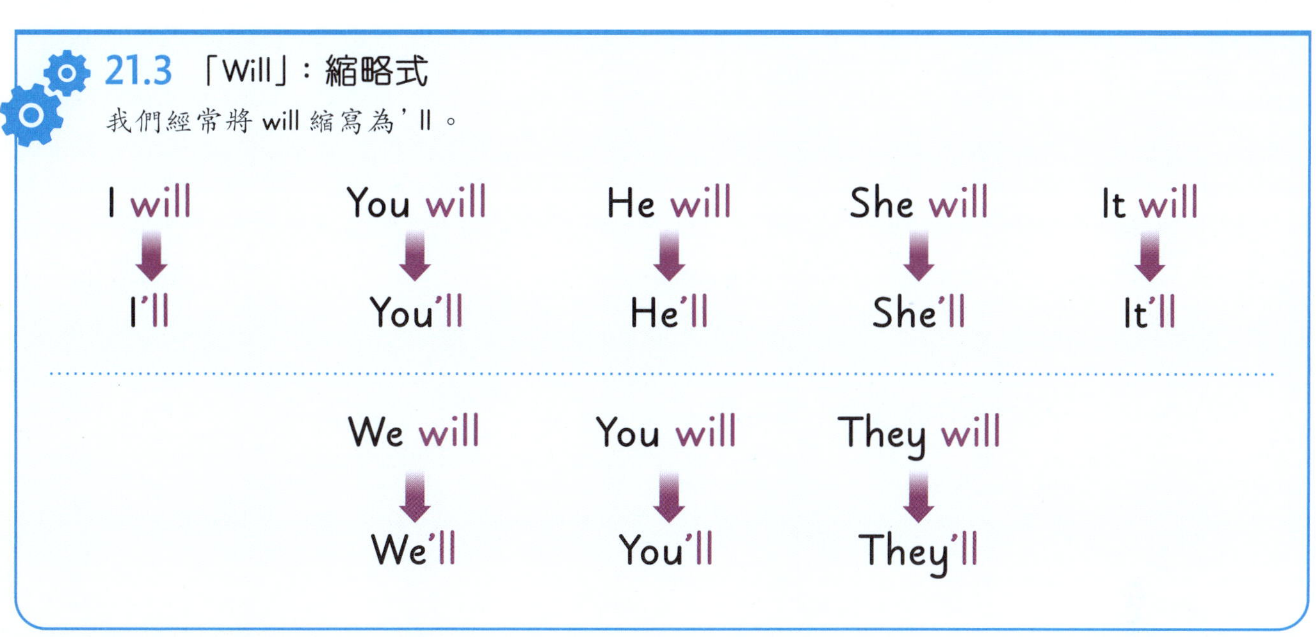

更多例子

I think you'll **like** this cake. It's chocolate!

That box looks heavy. I'll **carry** it for you.

I don't like the blue hat, so I'll **buy** the red one.

I'll **have** a burger.

We'll **be** home by 6 o'clock.

22 "Will" negatives

「Will」否定句

參見：
「Will」 第 21 單元
「Will」疑問句 第 23 單元

22.1 構成方法：「will」否定句

構成 will 否定句，在 will 後面加 not。

Amir **will** eat his dinner.

Amir **will not** eat his dinner.

將 not 放在 will 後面。

用法

除了第 21 單元的用法外，當某個人或某件事拒絕做某件事時，使用 will 否定句。

22.2 「Will」否定句：「will not」的縮略式

我們經常將 will not 縮寫為 won't。
Won't 對所有主語都保持不變。

更多例子

You **won't like** this comic book. It's boring!

I **won't be** late, I promise.

The dogs **will not come** inside.

23 "Will" questions

「Will」疑問句

參見：
「Will」 第 21 單元
構成疑問句 第 38 單元

23.1 構成方法：「will」疑問句

構成 will 疑問句，需將 will 放在主語前面。

You will be at the concert tomorrow.

Will you be at the concert tomorrow?

將 Will 放在主語 you 前面。

用法

使用 will 疑問句詢問未來的事情或請求他人做事情。

更多例子

Will you call me tomorrow?

Will it be a nice day tomorrow?

Will our team win the game?

Will you come to my birthday party?

Will you take a picture of us, please?

24 Present for future events

表示將來事件的現在式

24.1 構成方法：表示將來事件的簡單現在式

06:00

主語	動詞	時間標誌
The train	leaves	at 6 o'clock.

這個動詞使用簡單現在式，但描述的事件發生在將來。

時間標誌通常讓你知道該事件發生在將來。

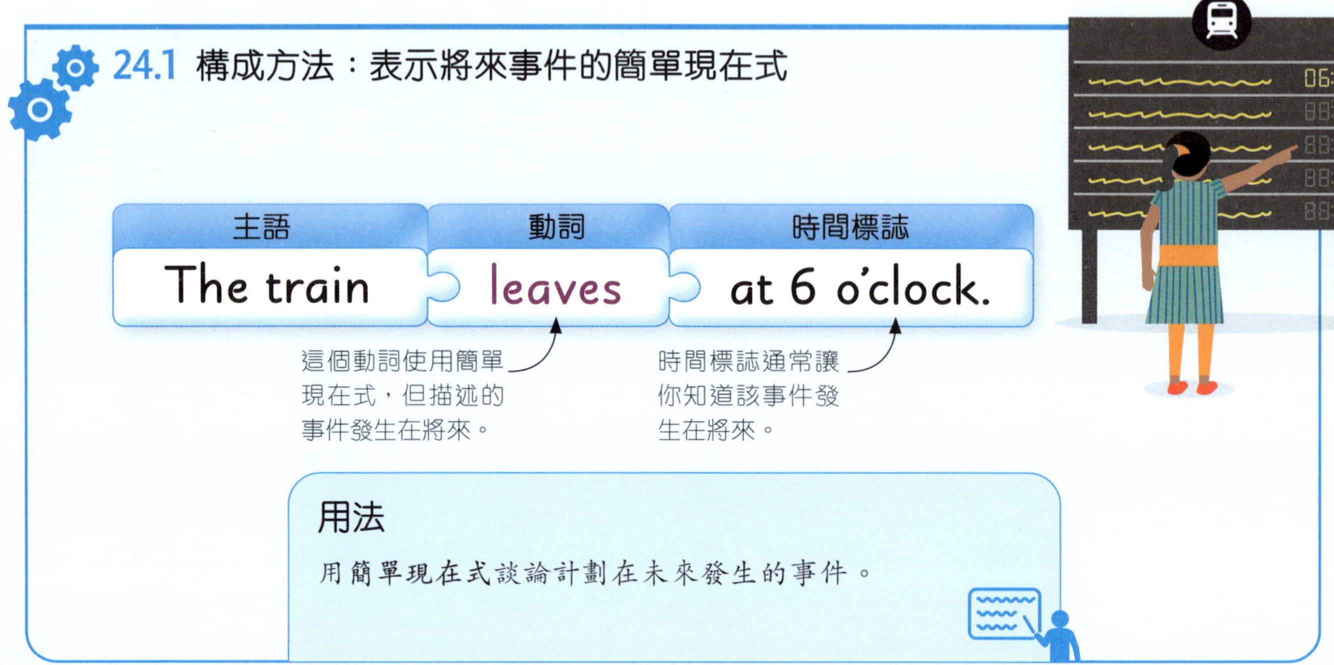

用法

用簡單現在式談論計劃在未來發生的事件。

更多例子

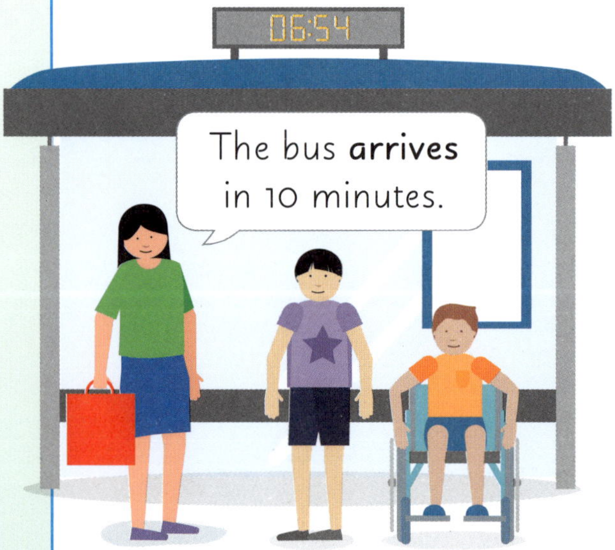

06:54
The bus **arrives** in 10 minutes.

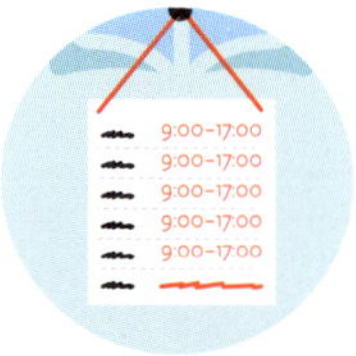

9:00–17:00
9:00–17:00
9:00–17:00
9:00–17:00
9:00–17:00

The shop **opens** at 9 o'clock.

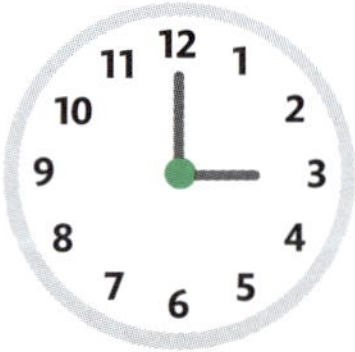

12
1
2
3
4
5
6
7
8
9
10
11

The film **starts** at 3 o'clock.

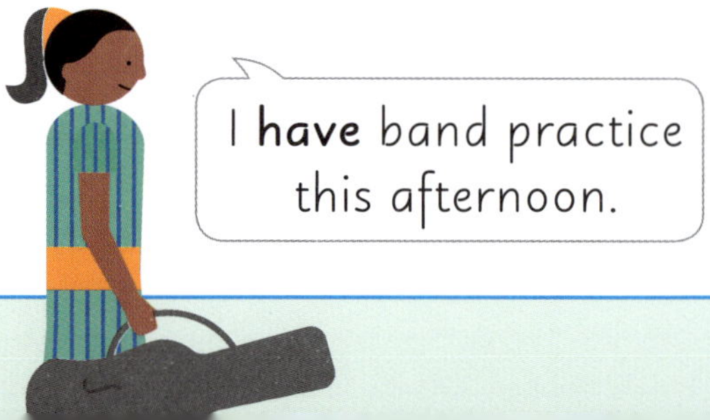

I **have** band practice this afternoon.

參見：
「Going to」 第 18 單元
「Will」 第 21 單元

24.2 構成方法：表示將來事件的現在進行式

主語	am/is/are	現在分詞	句子其他部分
I	am	having	pasta for dinner later.

根據主語使用 am、is 或 are。

使用主要動詞的現在分詞形式。

時間標誌通常會讓你知道該事件發生在將來。

用法

用現在進行式談論已計劃的未來事件。

更多例子

I'm **going** to the fair tomorrow.

They**'re playing** badminton after school.

We**'re flying** to Mexico next week.

注意！

想了解更多關於簡單現在式的構成，請參閱第 1 單元。想了解更多關於現在進行式的構成，請參閱第 4 單元。

25 Future tenses overview 將來式概述

我們會用 going to 和 will 預測未來，以及談論我們已做出的決定，但二者的使用場合不同。我們也會用現在式談論將來的事件。

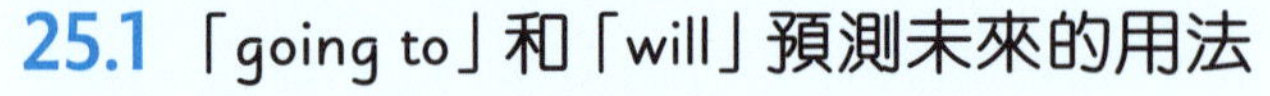

25.1 「going to」和「will」預測未來的用法

當前沒有任何證據時，用 will 對未來進行預測。

I think Sara will win the race.

比賽還未開始，所以沒有證據表明 Sara 會贏。

根據當前現有的證據，使用 going to 預測未來會發生的事情。

Look, Sara is going to win the race!

Sara 在前面，所以有證據表明她會贏得比賽。

注意！

我們也會用 will 作出承諾，以及主動提出為他人做事情。更多內容請參閱第 21 單元。

25.2 「going to」和「will」表達決定的用法

用 going to 談論你在現在這刻之前已經做出的決定。

提前作出這個決定。

I'm going to buy a present for Ben.

用 will 談論你剛才做出的決定。

在說話時快速作出這個決定。

I know! I will buy him a robot.

25.3 表示將來事件的現在式的用法

了解如何構成簡單現在式，請參閱第 1 單元。構成現在進行式，用 am 、is 或 are ，後面跟着現在分詞。更多內容請參閱第 4 單元。

The museum closes at 8 o'clock today.

We're having a party tonight.

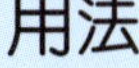

用法

用簡單現在式談論按計劃在將來發生的事件。

用現在進行式談論已經計劃好的未來事件。

26 Imperatives 祈使句

26.1 構成方法：祈使句

構成祈使句時，使用動詞基本形式。
祈使句沒有單數和複數形式的分別，也沒有禮貌或隨意形式的分別。

基本形式
Listen!

我們經常在祈使句後面使用感嘆號（exclamation mark）。

構成祈使句時，使用動詞基本形式。

基本形式	句子其他部分
Open	your books, please.

賓語可以放在祈使句後面。

加 please 使祈使句更禮貌。

用法

祈使句用於指示他人做事情。

參見：
不定式和基本形式　第 42 單元

26.2 構成方法：否定祈使句（negative imperatives）

構成否定祈使句，需在祈使動詞基本形式前面加 do not 或 don't。

Don't	基本形式
Don't	run!

告訴某個人不要做某件事，在動詞基本形式前面加 don't。

Don't	基本形式 + 請
Don't	run, please.

用法

用否定祈使句指示他人停止或不要做某件事情。

更多例子

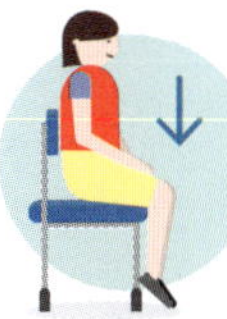

Sit down, please.

Be careful!

Stand up.

Don't touch that! It's hot.

Stop!

Don't talk, please.

Help!

Don't worry, it's OK.

27 「Let's」和「shall」

參見：
不定式和基本形式 第 42 單元

Let's take a photo!

27.1 構成方法：「let's」和「shall」

使用 let's 後面跟動詞基本形式。

Let's	基本形式	句子其他部分
Let's	take	a photo!

有時在 let's 句子的句尾使用感嘆號。

Let's 總是用這種縮寫形式。

Shall 後面跟着 I 或 we，再加基本形式。

Shall we take a photo?

用 Shall we 提出建議。

Shall I help you wash the dishes?

用 Shall I 或 shall we 主動提出做事情。

用法

用 let's 提出包括說話者在內的活動建議。用 shall 的疑問句提出建議或提議。

更多例子

Let's **read** a book!

Shall we go swimming?

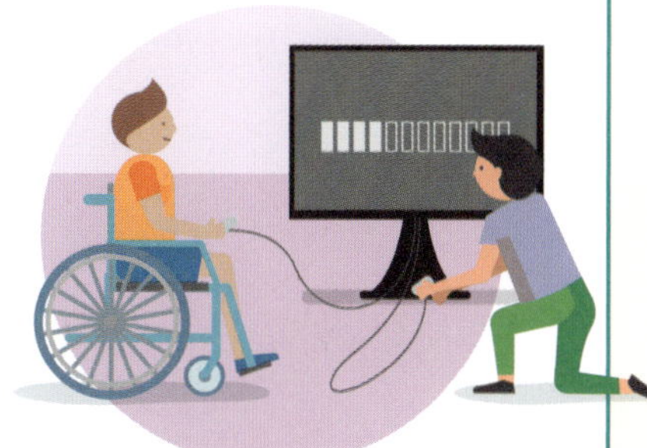

Let's play video games.

Shall I buy you an ice cream?

Let's play in the garden.

Let's go to the park!

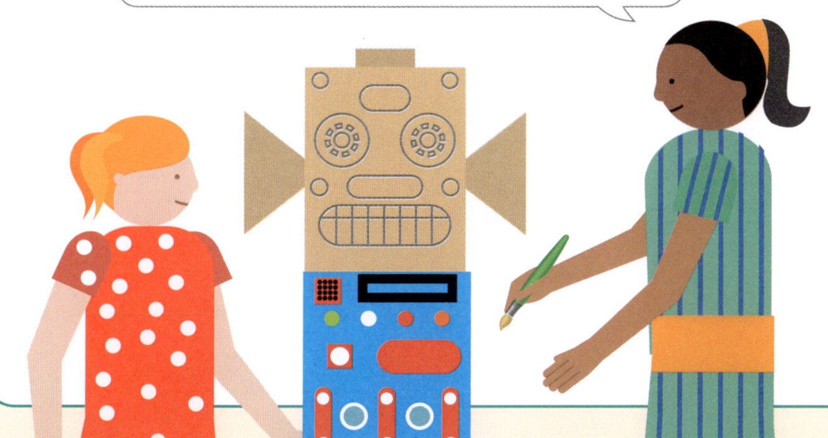

Let's sing and **dance**!

28 Modal verbs 情態動詞

參見：
簡短回答 第 39 單元
附加疑問句 第 41 單元

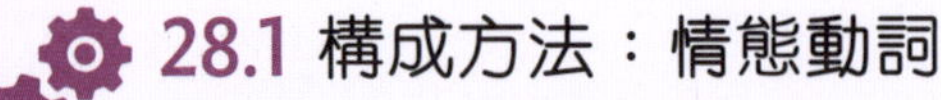

28.1 構成方法：情態動詞

情態動詞與普通動詞的用法不同，其形式不隨主語改變，後面通常跟着主要動詞基本形式。

主語	情態動詞	基本形式	句子其他部分
I You He She It We You They	can	catch	a ball.

情態動詞對所有主語都保持不變，he、she 或 it 後面不加 s。

主要動詞用基本形式。

28.2 構成方法：情態動詞否定句

構成情態動詞否定句，在後面加 not。

You should wear a coat.

You should not wear a coat.

在情態動詞後面加 not。

情態動詞的用法

情態動詞是英語中的特殊動詞，用於表達各種含義，例如可能性和義務等。

Ability 能力	can could	I **can** dance really well. Maria **could** write her name when she was four.
Requests 請求	can	**Can** I have an orange, please?
Permission 許可	can	**Can** we sit here?
Advice 建議	should	It's very sunny. You **should** wear a hat.
Suggestions 建議	could	You **could** draw a picture of a flower.
Possibility 可能性	might may could	We **might** go to the zoo today. I **may** be late to the party. Don't go outside. You **could** get wet.
Obligations 義務	must	I **must** remember to do my homework.

28.3 構成方法：情態動詞疑問句

構成情態動詞疑問句時，將情態動詞放在主語前面。

將情態動詞放在主語前面。

29 "Can" for ability
「Can」表示能力

29.1 構成方法：「can」表示現在的能力

Can 是情態動詞，後面跟着動詞基本形式。 Can 對所有主語都保持不變，he、she 或 it 後面不加 s。

主語	can	基本形式	句子其他部分
I	can	play	the piano.

主要動詞用基本形式。

用法

用 can 描述人物或事物現有的能力。

29.2 構成方法：「can」否定句

Can 否定句在 can 後面加 not，構成否定句 cannot。我們經常將 cannot 縮寫為 can't。兩者都對所有主語都保持不變。

I can play the piano.

I cannot play the piano.

cannot 是一個單字，我們經常縮寫為 can't。

用法

用 cannot 或 can't 談論人物或事物不能做的事情。

29.3 構成方法：「can」疑問句

用 can 提問時，將 can 放在主語前面。

You can play the piano.

Can you play the piano?

Can 放在主語前面。

用法

用 can 疑問句詢問他人或事物是否能夠做某事。

參見：
「Can」表示請求和許可　第 30 單元
「Could」表示建議　第 33 單元

更多例子

They **can read**.

It **can catch** a ball.

The tortoise **cannot walk** fast.

He **can't sing** very well.

She **can't hear** the music.

Can he ski?

Can she ride a bike?

29.4 構成方法：「could」表示過去的能力

Could 是 can 的過去式，後面使用主要動詞基本形式。Could 對所有主語都保持不變，he、she 或 it 後面不加 s。

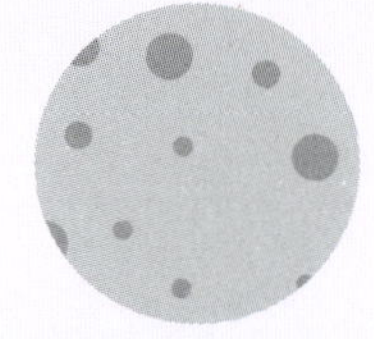

主語	could	基本形式	句子其他部分
We	could	see	the moon last night.

could 對所有主語都保持不變。

用法

用 could 談論人物或事物過去能夠做的事情。

29.5 構成方法：「could」否定句

構成 could 的否定句時，在後面加 not，我們經常將 could not 縮寫為 couldn't。

We could see the moon last night.

We could not see the moon last night.

將 not 放在 could 後面。

我們經常將 could not 縮寫為 couldn't。

用法

用 could not 或 couldn't 談論人物或事物過去不能做的事情。

29.6 構成方法：「could」疑問句

用 could 提問時，將 could 放在主語前面。

You could see the moon last night.

Could you see the moon last night?

將 Could 放在主語前面。

用法

用 could 疑問句詢問他人或事物過去是否能夠做某事。

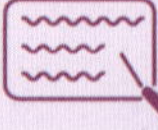

更多例子

He **could hear** the birds singing.

Maria **could understand** all the teacher's questions.

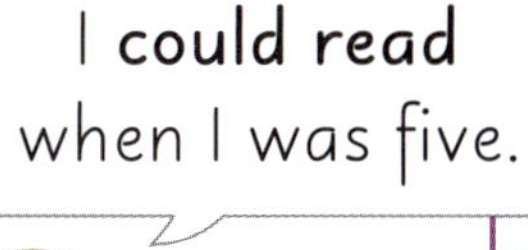

I **couldn't ride** my bike last week. It was broken.

We **couldn't visit** the museum yesterday because it was closed.

Andy **couldn't lift** the box because it was too heavy.

Could you swim when you were four?

Could Dad snowboard when he was a child?

Could you answer all the questions on the maths test?

30 "Can" for requests and permission

「Can」表示請求和許可

參見：
情態動詞 第 28 單元
「Can」表示能力 第 29 單元

Can I have an apple, please?

Yes, you can.

30.1 構成方法：「can」表示請求和許可

Can 是情態動詞，在所有主語後面都保持不變。
用 can 提問時，將 can 放在主語前面。

Can	主語	基本形式	句子其他部分
Can	I	have	an apple, please?
	we		

我們通常用 I 或 we 提出請求或詢問許可。

30.2 「Can」表示請求和許可的用法

Can I have a pear, please?

Can 在所有主語後面都保持不變。

用法

用 can 提出請求。

Can we play outside?

Can 後面跟着動詞基本形式。

用 can 詢問做事情的許可。

更多例子

Can I buy a new toy?

Can we play football?

Can we go to the fair?

Can we have some juice, please?

Can I hold your rabbit?

Can I eat a biscuit?

Can I have an ice cream?

Can we visit Grandma again soon?

Can I wear my new dress tonight?

31 「Must」、「have to」和「have got to」

參見：
簡單現在式　第 1 單元
情態動詞　第 28 單元

I must go now, my dinner is ready.

31.1 構成方法：「must」、「have to」和「have got to」

Must 是情態動詞，後面跟着動詞基本形式。
Must 對所有主語都保持不變。
在 he 、 she 和 it 後， have to 變為 has to ，have got to 變為 has got to 。

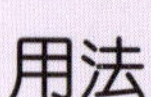

主語	must/have to/have got to	基本形式
I You	must have to have got to	go.
He She It	must has to has got to	go.
We You They	must have to have got to	go.

用法

用 must 、 have to 或 have got to 表示需要做的事情。

更多例子

I **must wear** a coat because it's raining.

Andy **has to eat** all his vegetables.

I **have to get up** for school now.

Sofia **has got to tidy** her room.

He **must finish** his letter before dinner.

She**'s got to practise** her trumpet.

注意！

在包括 have to 的句子中，不能將 have to 縮寫為 've to，也不能將 has to 縮寫為 's to。

We **must run** to catch the bus.

They **have to wear** a uniform to school.

31.2 構成方法：「must」否定句

Must 否定句，將 not 放在 must 後面。
我們有時可以將 must not 縮寫為 mustn't 。

You must be careful in science class.

You must not touch the fire.

在 must 後面加 not 。

用法

用 must not 或 mustn't 表示不被允許做某事。

注意！

Must 和 have to 或 have got to 否定句的意思不同。

更多例子

You **mustn't drop** litter.

You **must not use** a calculator in the test.

You **must not swim** in the sea today.

31.3 構成方法：「have to」和「have got to」否定句

Have to 否定句，在 have 或 has 前面加 do not 或 does not，並將 has 還原為基本形式 have。
我們通常將 do not 縮寫為 don't，以及將 does not 縮寫為 doesn't。

She **has to go** to school on Mondays.

She **does not have to go** to school at the weekend.

在 have 或 has 前面加 do not 或 does not。

have 是 to have 的基本形式。

構成 have got to 否定句，需將 not 放在 have 或 has 後面。
我們經常將 have not 縮寫為 haven't，以及將 has not 縮寫為 hasn't。

She **has got to walk** to school today.

She **has not got to walk** to school today.

將 not 放在 have 或 has 後面。

用法

當你不需要做事情，或可以做非必要的事情時，使用 do not have to 或 have not got to。

更多例子

Sofia **doesn't have to leave** the party yet.

You **haven't got to go** to bed yet.

31.4 構成方法：「have」和「have got to」疑問句

我們通常不用 must 來提問。用 have to 提問時，在主語前面加 do 或 does，並將 has 還原為基本形式 have。

He has to go to bed.

Does he have to go to bed?

I、you、we 或 they 使用 do。
He、she 或 it 使用 does。

用法

用 have to 或 have got to 疑問句詢問他人需要做的事情。

用 have got to 提問時，將 have 或 has 放在主語前面。

He has got to go to bed.

Has he got to go to bed?

將 has 放在主語 he 前面。

更多例子

Do I have to take a hat with me?

Does he have to stay at home today?

Do they have to wear a uniform to work?

31.5 構成方法：「have to」過去式

Must 與 have got to 沒有過去式。Have to 的過去式是 had to。Had to 後面跟着動詞基本形式。Had to 對所有主語都保持不變。He、she 或 it 後面不加 s。

用法

用 had to 描述過去必須做的事。

主語	had to	基本形式	句子其他部分
I	had to	clean	my boots after football.

had to 對所有主語都保持不變。

更多例子

I **had to get up** early yesterday.

He **had to answer** ten questions on the test.

They **had to paint** a picture today.

We **had to catch** a bus into town because my bike was broken.

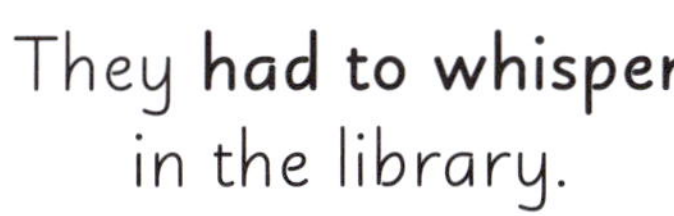

They **had to whisper** in the library.

32 "Might", "May" and "Could" for possibility

「Might」、「may」和「could」表示可能性

參見：
情態動詞 第 28 單元
「Can」表示能力 第 29 單元

We might go to the fair today, but we're not sure.

32.1 構成方法：「might」和「may」表示可能性

Might 和 may 是情態動詞，後面跟着動詞基本形式。
Might 和 may 對所有主語都保持不變，he 、 she 或 it 後面不加 s 。

主語	might/may	基本形式	句子其他部分
We	might may	go	to the fair today.

Might 與 may 意思相同。

用法

使用 might 或 may 談論可能正在發生或即將發生的事情，或不確定的事情。

32.2 構成方法：「might」與「may」否定句

構成 might 或 may 的否定句，將 not 放在 might 或 may 後面。

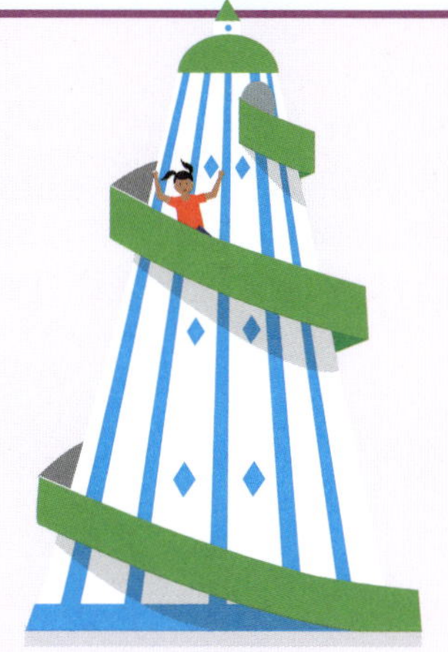

We **might go** to the fair today.

We **might not go** to the fair today.

將 not 放在 might 或 may 後面。

更多例子

The cat **may be** asleep.

They **might play** a board game later.

He **might not hit** the ball.

Andy **may not go** to school today because he is ill.

She **might paint** a picture of a house.

Look at those clouds. It **might rain**.

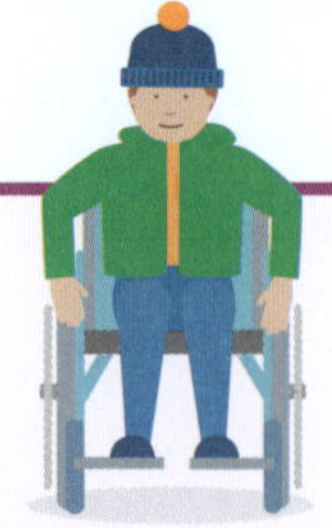

32.3 構成方法：「could」表示可能性

Could 是情態動詞，後面跟着基本形式。
Could 對所有主語都保持不變，he 、 she 或 it 後面不加 s 。

主語	could	基本形式	句子其他部分
It	could	snow	today. It's very cold.

Could 對所有主語都保持不變。

用法

用 could 談論可能發生或成真的事情，它的否定形式 can't 不適用於此語境。

更多例子

Andy is very tired. He **could fall** asleep.

Don't drop that! It **could break**.

They're playing really well. They **could win** the game!

Cycling without a helmet **could be** dangerous.

33 「Could」for suggestions
「Could」表示建議

參見：
情態動詞 第 28 單元
「Can」表示能力 第 29 單元

You could play a game.

33.1 構成方法：「Could」表示建議

Could 是情態動詞，後面跟着動詞基本形式。Could 對所有主語都保持不變，he、she 或 it 後面不加 s。

用法

用 could 提出建議，你可以用 or 提出一個或多個選擇。

主語	could	基本形式	句子其他部分
You	could	play	a game.

Could 對所有主語都保持不變

更多例子

Maria **could wear** her new shoes to Grandma's today.

It's a sunny day. We **could go** to the beach or the lake.

I'm cold!

You **could put on** a jumper.

34「Should」

參見：
情態動詞　第 28 單元
「Could」表示建議　第 33 單元

It's windy today. You should wear a coat.

34.1 構成方法：「should」

Should 是情態動詞，後面跟着基本形式。
Should 對所有主語都保持不變，he 、 she 或 it 後面不加 s 。

主語	should	基本形式	句子其他部分
You	should	wear	a coat.

should 對所有主語都保持不變。

用法

用 should 提供或尋求建議。

34.2 構成方法：「should」否定句和疑問句

構成 should 否定句，在 should 後面加 not 。我們經常將 should not 縮寫為 shouldn't 。

You should go outside.

You should not go outside.

構成 should 疑問句，需把 should 放在主語前面。

We should take an umbrella.

Should we take an umbrella?

將 Should 放在主語 we 前面。

更多例子

It's 7 o'clock. Maria **should get up**.

The puppy **shouldn't eat** that!

Should we buy some cereal for our camping trip?

It's very hot today. You **should drink** lots of water.

Amy **shouldn't stay up** late. She has got school tomorrow.

They **should go** camping in the summer when it's warm.

Should Sara bake a cake or some biscuits?

35 「Would like」

參見：
不定式和基本形式 第 42 單元
名詞 第 50 單元

I **would like** an ice cream.

I **would like** to go to the park.

35.1 構成方法：「would like」

Would 是情態動詞。Would 後面跟着 like 的基本形式，構成 would like。Would like 對所有主語都保持不變，後面可跟着名詞或 to 的不定式（infinitive）動詞。

主語	would like	名詞
I	would like	an ice cream.

主語	would like	不定式	句子其他部分
I	would like	to go	to the park.

當與動詞連用時，would like 後面跟着 to 的不定式。

用法

使用 would like 加名詞，禮貌地請求某物。

使用 would like 加動詞，禮貌地表達想做的事情。

更多例子

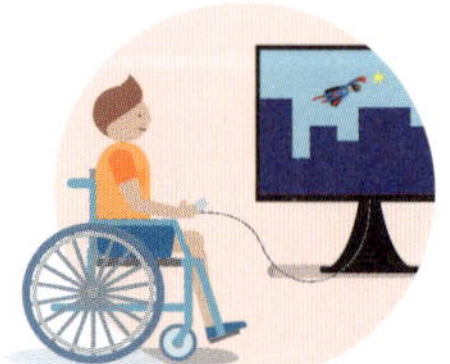

Ben **would like** to play a game.

I **would like** another glass of juice, please.

He'**d like** to read a book.

35.2 構成方法：「would like」疑問句

構成包括 would like 疑問句，需將 would 放在主語前面。

You would like an ice cream.

Would you like an ice cream?

將 Would 放在主語 you 前面。

like 保持在相同的位置。

用法

使用 would like 和名詞的疑問句，禮貌地詢問他人是否想要某物。

You would like to go to the park.

Would you like to go to the park?

使用 would like 和不定式的疑問句，禮貌地詢問他人是否想做某事。

更多例子

提示！

你可以將 would 縮寫為 'd。

I would like → I'd like

前往 R20 了解更多資訊。

Would you like to play with me?

Would you like an apple?

Would you like to draw a picture?

Would you like some help with your homework?

36 Zero conditional
零條件句

參見：
簡單現在式 第 1 單元
祈使句 第 26 單元

When it snows,
we build a snowman.

36.1 構成方法：零條件句

構成零條件句時，用 if 或 when 後面跟着一個動作或情況，然後加該動作或情況的結果，兩部分都用簡單現在式。

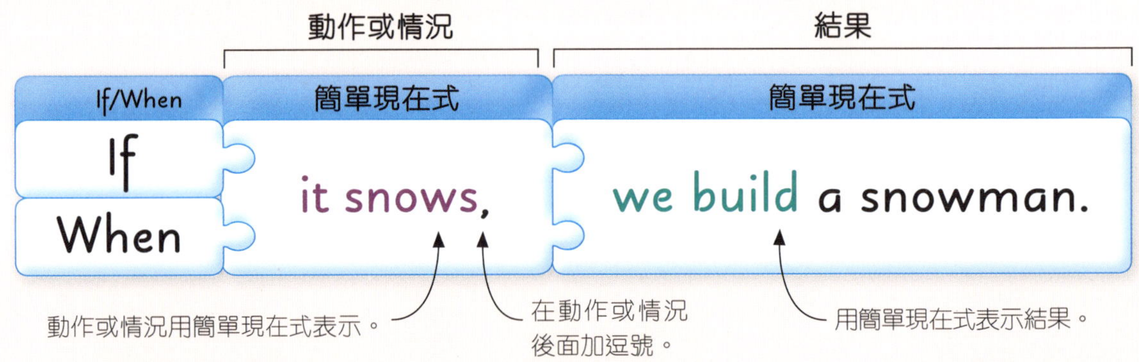

你可以將結果移到動作或情況前面來構成句子。
用這種方式構成句子時不用逗號。

沒有逗號。

用法

用零條件句談論作為動作或情況的結果，而總是發生的事情。

36.2 構成方法：帶祈使句的零條件句

你可以在零條件句後面跟着祈使句。

用法

使用帶祈使句的零條件句告訴他人發生某個動作或情況時，他們應該做甚麼。

提示！

你可以將建議的動作放在動作或情況前面。這樣做不需要加逗號。

更多例子

I **play** with my toys if **I'm bored**.

When **it rains, we can't play** in the garden.

When **I'm tired**, **I go** to bed early.

When **the dog is hungry**, **give** it some food.

If **you're thirsty**, **drink** some water.

Go to the doctor if **you're ill**.

37 First conditional
第一條件句

參見：
簡單現在式 第 1 單元
「Will」 第 21 單元

If we win the competition,
we'll get a trophy.

37.1 構成方法：第一條件句

構成第一條件句時，if 後面跟着一個簡單現在式的動作或情況，然後用 will 表示結果。

	可能的動作或情況	未來的結果
If	簡單現在式	will
If	we win the competition,	we'll get a trophy.

用簡單現在式表示動作或情況。

在動作或情況後面加逗號。

結果用 will 表示。

你可以通過將未來的結果移到可能發生的動作或情況之前來構成句子。用這種方式構成句子時，不用加逗號。

If we win the competition, we'll get a trophy.

We'll get a trophy if we win the competition.

沒有逗號。

記住！

我們經常將 will 縮寫為 'll。前往 21.3 了解更多資訊。

用法

第一條件句用於描述可能發生的情況和預期結果。

更多例子

If I **drop** this,
it will break.

You'll feel better if
you take this medicine.

If I **tidy** my room,
Mum will be happy.

He'll fall off if
he's not careful.

If **it's sunny** tomorrow,
we'll go to the beach.

If **we get** a dog,
we'll walk it every day.

They'll win the game if **he catches** the ball!

38 Forming questions
構成疑問句

構成疑問句的方式有兩種：將動詞放在主語前面，或使用 do 、 does 或 did 。

參見：
簡單現在式 第 1 單元
疑問詞 第 40 單元

38.1 構成方法：簡單現在式疑問句

在簡單現在式疑問句中，不是 to be 、 to have got 或情態動詞時，需使用 do 或 does ，並使用主要動詞基本形式，不要在主要動詞後面加 s 。

She likes board games.

Does she like board games?

加 Do 或 Does 。

主要動詞保持基本形式。

38.2 構成方法：簡單過去式疑問句

在簡單過去式疑問句中，不是 to be 的動詞，需使用 did ，並使用主要動詞基本形式，不要使用動詞的過去式， did 對所有主語都適用。

He played basketball.

Did he play basketball?

將 Did 放在問題開頭。

主要動詞保持基本形式。

38.3 構成方法：「to be」簡單現在式疑問句

構成 to be 簡單現在式疑問句，需將 am 、 is 或 are 放在主語前面。

38.4 構成方法：「to be」簡單過去式疑問句

構成 to be 簡單過去式疑問句，需將 was 或 were 放在主語前面。

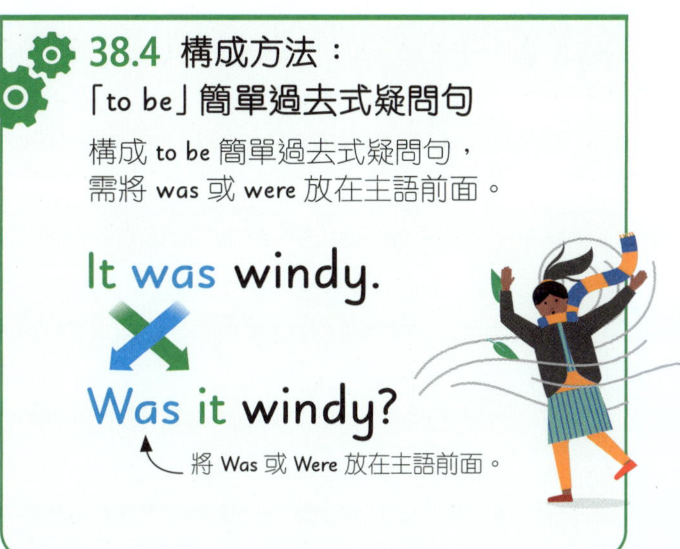

38.5 構成方法：情態動詞疑問句

構成情態動詞疑問句，需將情態動詞放在主語前面，以及主要動詞的位置保持不變。

38.6 構成方法：現在完成式疑問句

構成現在完成式疑問句，需將 have 或 has 放在主語前面，過去分詞在原位置保持不變。

39 Short answers 簡短回答

回答問題時可省略部分詞語，這種回答稱為簡短回答，在英語口語中非常常見。

39.1 構成方法：「to be」簡短回答

如果問題以 to be 開頭，簡短回答中使用相同時態的 to be 。

39.2 構成方法：「to do」簡短回答

如果問題以 do 、 does 或 did 開頭，簡短回答中使用相同形式的助動詞。

更多例子

Is it your tortoise?
Yes, **it is**.

Were you at school yesterday?
Yes, **we were**.

Was he studying English?
No, **he wasn't**.

更多例子

Do you like apples?
Yes, **I do**.

Does he wake up early?
No, **he doesn't**.

Did you win the game?
Yes, **we did**!

參見：
情態動詞 第 28 單元
構成疑問句 第 38 單元

39.3 構成方法：「to have」簡短回答

如果問題以 have 或 has 開頭，簡短回答中使用相同形式的 have。

更多例子

Has he bought a fish?
Yes, **he has**.

Have we got to leave?
Yes, **we have**.

Have they finished their dinner?
No, **they haven't**.

39.4 構成方法：情態動詞簡短回答

如果問題以情態動詞開頭，簡短回答中使用相同的情態動詞。

更多例子

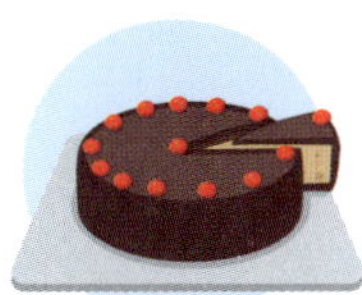

Would you like a piece of cake?
Yes, **I would**.

Should she clean her boots?
Yes, **she should**.

Can we watch TV?
No, **you can't**.

40 Question words 疑問詞

我們使用疑問詞提出無法用簡單 yes 或 no 回答的問題。

參見：
構成疑問句 第 38 單元

40.1 「Who」誰

用 who 詢問關於人的問題。

40.2 「Whose」誰的

用 whose 詢問事物是誰的。

40.3 「Where」哪裏

用 where 詢問關於地點、方向或人、事物位置的問題。

40.4 「When」甚麼時候

用 when 詢問關於時間的問題。

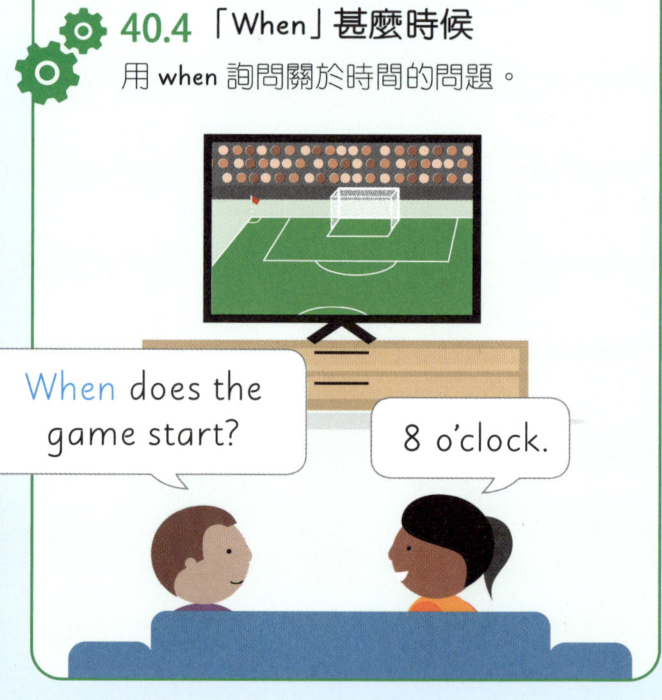

40.5「What」甚麼

用 what 詢問關於事物的問題。

40.6「Which」哪個

用 which 讓人物在兩個或多個指定事物中做出選擇。

40.7「What」and「which」甚麼和哪個

用 what 詢問關於事物的一般問題，用 which 詢問兩個或多個選擇的問題。

40.8「Why」為甚麼

用 why 詢問原因。

40.9「How」怎樣

用 how 詢問事情的細節，或做事情的方式。

40.10「How often」多久一次

用 how often 詢問他人做事情的頻率。

40.11「How many」多少

用 how many 詢問可數名詞的數量（quantity）。

40.12「How much」多少

用 how much 詢問不可數名詞的數量。

更多例子

Who 誰	用於詢問關於人的問題。	**Who** caught the ball? **Who** is winning the race?
Whose 誰的	用於詢問事物是誰的。	**Whose** jacket is this? **Whose** dog is called Spot?
Where 哪裏	用於詢問地點、方向或位置。	**Where** do you live? **Where** is she going?
When 甚麼時候	用於詢問時間。	**When** do you get up in the morning? **When** are we going to go on holiday?
What 甚麼	用於詢問事物。	**What** is your name? **What** is the time?
Which 哪個	用於讓人物在兩個或多個事物中選擇。	**Which** do you prefer, cats or dogs? **Which** coat is yours?
Why 為甚麼	用於詢問原因。	**Why** is he laughing? **Why** are you late?
How 怎樣	用於詢問細節或做事的方式。	**How** do you spell "kitchen"? **How** did you get to school?
How often 多久一次	用於詢問做事情的頻率。	**How often** do you play basketball? **How often** do they go to the beach?
How many 多少（可數）	用於詢問可數名詞的數量。	**How many** balloons are there? **How many** birds can you see?
How much 多少（不可數）	用於詢問不可數名詞的數量。	**How much** cake is there? **How much** juice would you like?

41 Tag questions 附加疑問句

參見：
情態動詞 第 28 單元
構成疑問句 第 38 單元

The grey dog is very big, isn't it?

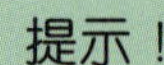

提示！
對於含有 I am 的陳述句，其否定附加疑問句用 aren't I。

41.1 構成方法：附加疑問句

附加疑問句是在陳述句的句尾加簡短問題。
如果陳述句是肯定的（positive statement），附加疑問句用否定形式。

肯定陳述句	否定附加疑問句
The grey dog is very big,	isn't it?

動詞是肯定的。 附加疑問句是否定的。

如果陳述句是否定的，使用肯定的附加疑問句。

否定陳述句	肯定附加疑問句
The brown dog isn't very big,	is it?

這個動詞是否定的。 附加疑問句是肯定的。

用法

使用附加疑問句邀請他認同你的觀點，或詢問你剛才所說的內容是否正確。

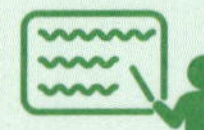

41.2 附加疑問句的用法

帶有 to be 的句子，使用 to be 在附加疑問句中。

It is really hot today, isn't it?

這個動詞是 to be。 附加疑問句中的動詞是 to be。

41.3 附加疑問句使用其他動詞的用法

你所使用的附加疑問句類型取決於句子第一部分中的動詞。

對於大多數簡單現在式的動詞，使用 do 、 does 、 don't 或 doesn't 。

You love dancing, don't you?

對於大多數簡單過去式的動詞，使用 did 或 didn't 。

Ben played basketball today, didn't he?

對於情態動詞，附加疑問句中使用相同的情態動詞。

We shouldn't go outside, should we?

當 have 用於現在完成式，或包括 to have got 和 to have got to 的短語時，附加疑問句中使用 to have 。

You haven't read this book, have you?

41.4 表達方法：附加疑問句

附加疑問句有兩種表達的語調。
當附加疑問句需要回答時，句尾語調上揚。

You are coming to my party, aren't you?

當你只是讓某人認同你的觀點，以及附加疑問句不需要回答時，句尾語調下降。

語調下降。

That game was really fun, wasn't it?

42 Infinitives and base forms

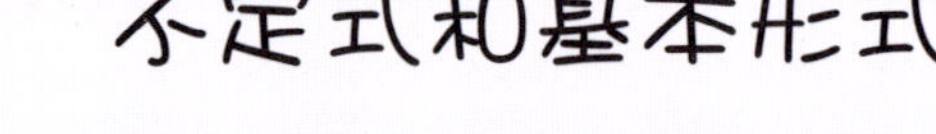

參見：
動名詞 第 43 單元
動詞形式 第 44 單元

42.1 不定式和基本形式

不定式和基本形式是英語動詞最簡單的形式。
不定式總是以 to 開頭，有時稱為「to - Infinitives」。
動詞基本形式與不定式相同，但不加 to 。

主語	動詞	不定式
I	like	to read.

不定式總是以 to 開頭

主語	動詞	基本形式	句子其他部分
I	should	read	more books.

這是基本形式動詞，沒有 to 。

用法

我們很少單獨使用不定式和基本形式，但會用它們來構成各種句子。

更多例子

I need **to tidy** my room.

Dad decided **to cook** pasta for dinner.

Sara can **ride** a bike.

We should **go** inside because we're too wet!

43 Gerunds 動名詞

參見：
不定式和基本形式 第 42 單元
動詞形式 第 44 單元

43.1 動名詞

動名詞是具名詞功能的動詞。

用法

用動名詞表達你對某項活動的感受。

更多例子

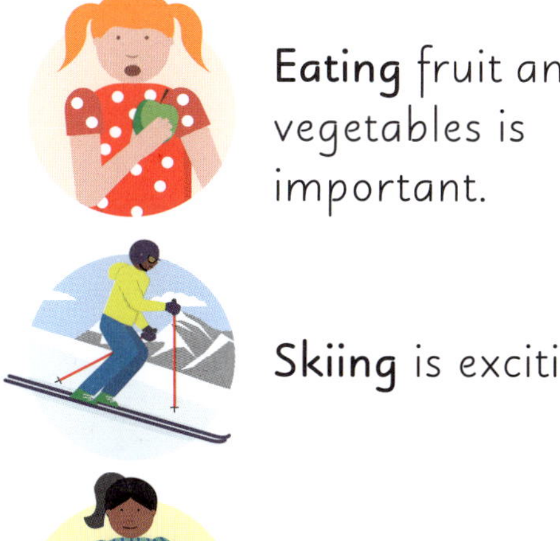

Eating fruit and vegetables is important.

Skiing is exciting!

I love **baking**. It's my favourite hobby.

43.2 拼寫規則：動名詞

構成動名詞，在動詞基本形式後面加 ing。

wear → wearing

大多數動詞加 ing。

有時，動詞基本形式的拼寫在加 ing 之前會發生變化。

最後一個字母是不發音的 e。

choose → choosing

去掉 e，然後加 ing。

最後兩個字母是 ie。

tie → tying

將 ie 改成 y，然後加 ing。

最後一個音節重音，且最後三個字母為子音、母音、子音的組合。

44 Verb patterns 動詞形式

參見：
不定式和基本形式　第 42 單元
動名詞　第 43 單元

44.1 構成方法：帶不定式和動名詞的動詞形式

有些動詞後面只能跟着不定式或動名詞，
而有些動詞後面兩者皆可，而且意思沒有分別。

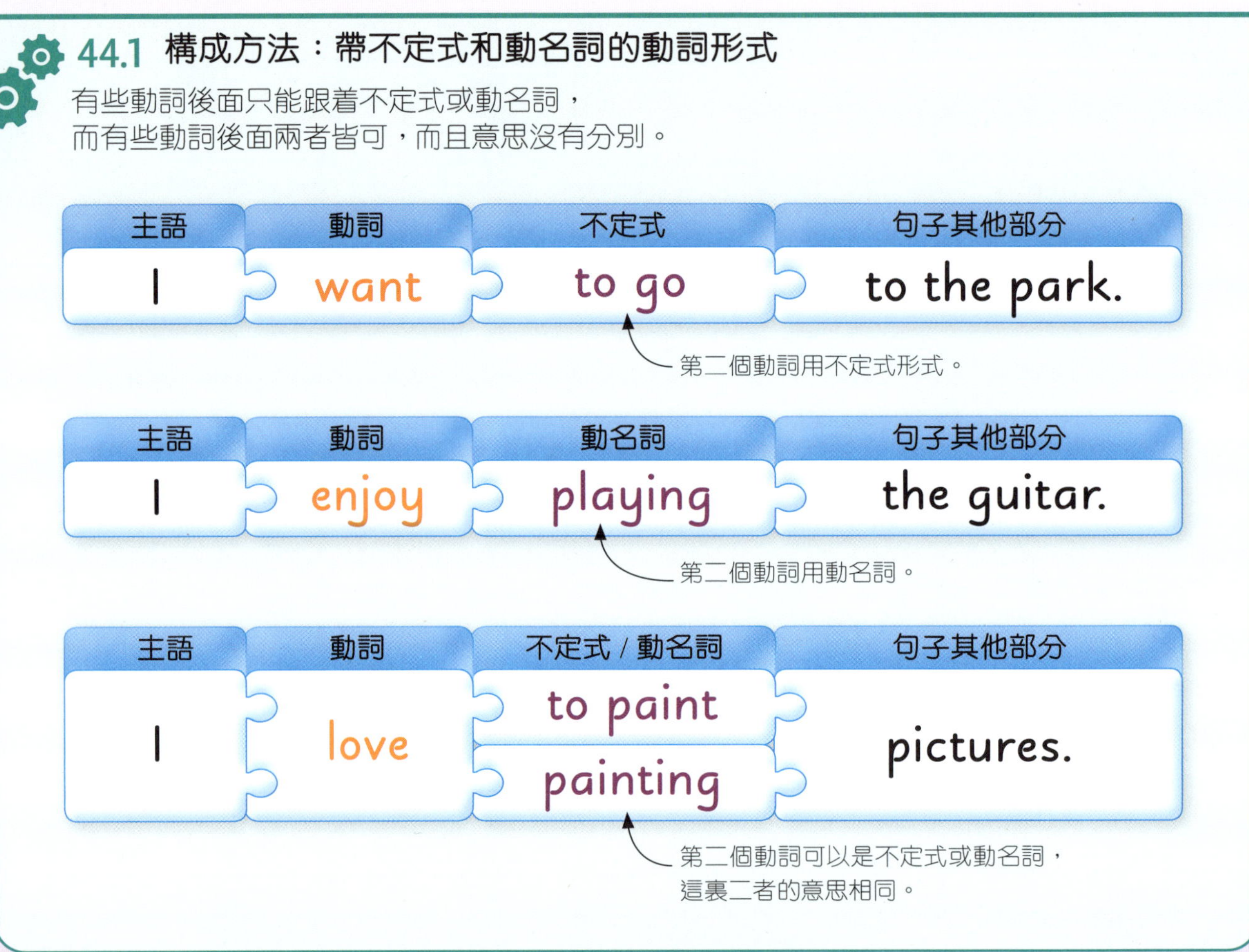

44.2 後面跟着不定式、動名詞或兩者皆可的動詞

動詞＋不定式		動詞＋動名詞		動詞＋不定式或動名詞	
agree	help	complete	keep	begin	love
ask	hope	dislike	miss	continue	prefer
choose	learn	enjoy	practise	hate	start
decide	want	finish	understand	like	

44.3 構成方法：帶賓語的動詞形式

當動詞 to have 後面跟着不定式時，你可以在 to have 和不定式之間加一個賓語。

主語	have/has	賓語	不定式
I	have	a story	to write.

用法

使用這種動詞形式談論你能或需要做的事情。

更多例子

She **is learning to spell**.

Max **decided to buy** a blue ball.

Ben **likes to play** with his car.

Maria **has finished eating** her dinner.

They **practise speaking** English every day.

Sara **likes riding** her bike.

Sofia **has** two **bags to carry**.

We **have** a **bus to catch**.

I **have ten questions to answer**.

45 Articles 冠詞

參見：
名詞 第 50 單元
最高級形容詞 第 65 單元

45.1 不定冠詞 (indefinite articles)

A 、 an 和 some 為不定冠詞。

I'd like a pear.

以子音開頭的單數名詞前面用 a 。

I'd like an apple.

以母音開頭的單數名詞前面用 an 。

I'd like some mangoes.

複數名詞或不可數名詞前面使用 some 。

用法

不定冠詞用於籠統地談論或首次提及的事物。

45.2 「Any」疑問句和否定句

在疑問句和否定句中，不定冠詞 some 變為 any 。

There are some bananas.

↓

Are there any bananas?

There are some bananas.

↓

There aren't any bananas.

更多例子

That's **a** nice drawing.

My dad is **an** actor.

There aren't **any** biscuits in the jar.

There is **some** milk in the fridge.

We need **some** flour for this cake.

Would you like **an** orange?

45.3 定冠詞（definite article）

The 是定冠詞。

I'm in **the** garden.

花園是一個特定的地方，所以用 the。

用法

用 the 談論特定的事物或地方。

用不定冠詞談論首次提及的事物。

We have **a** dog, **a** rabbit, and **a** tortoise. **The** dog is called Rex.

使用 the 是因為這隻狗已經被提及過了。

用 the 談論已經提過的事物。

Rex is **the** biggest.

在最高級前面使用 the。

在最高級形容詞或副詞前面使用 the。

更多例子

Max is **the** fastest in our school.

We are washing **the** car.

I loved **the** clown at Maria's party.

I can see a butterfly and a ladybird. **The** butterfly is blue.

45.4 比較不定冠詞和定冠詞

My favourite animal is **a** frog.

我們使用不定冠詞，因為我們在泛指青蛙。

我們使用定冠詞，因為我們在談論一隻特定的青蛙。

The frog in our garden is green.

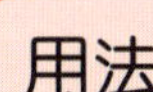

用法

用不定冠詞來談論泛指的事物，用定冠詞來談論特定的事物。

更多例子

Maria would like **a** biscuit.

The biscuits at the party were delicious!

I'm going to buy **a** new toy car.

The toy car in the shop is expensive.

46 「This」、「that」、「these」、「those」

46.1 指示限定詞 (demonstrative determiners)

This 、 that 、 these 和 those 可以用在名詞前面，指明你所談論的具體事物。當它們起到這個作用時，就是指示限定詞。

This robot is green.

用法

在附近的單數名詞或不可數名詞前面使用 this 。

That robot is red.

在遠處的單數名詞或不可數名詞前面使用 that 。

These robots are green.

在附近的複數名詞前面使用 these 。

Those robots are red.

在遠處的複數名詞前面使用 those 。

參見：
名詞 第 50 單元
所有格形容詞 第 55 單元

更多例子

I love **this** dress!

This music is great.

This pear is delicious.

Ben would like to use **that** computer.

That elephant is very big!

That game looks fun.

Have you tried **these** cakes?

I've read all **these** books.

These flowers smell lovely.

Those children are playing in the park.

Can you see **those** lions?

Look at **those** kites!

46.2 名詞指示代詞 (demonstrative pronouns)

This、that、these 和 those 可以在句子中代替名詞，此時它們就是指示代詞。

This is my cat.

This cat is my cat.

This is my cat.

用法

用 this 代替附近的單數或不可數名詞。

That is your cat.

我們經常將 that is 縮寫為 that's。

用 that 代替遠處的單數或不可數名詞。

These are my cats.

用 these 代替附近的複數名詞。

Those are your cats.

用 those 代替遠處的複數名詞。

更多例子

This tastes great!

Is **this** your jumper?

Can you hold **this** for me, please?

That is a nice bag.

That's a very cute dog.

I think **that**'s broken.

These are my dolls.

These are my new shoes.

Are **these** your pencils?

Those are the sandwiches for my party.

Those are my paintings.

Are **those** for me?

47「Another」

參見：
「Both」第 48 單元
數字 第 61 單元

Can I have another apple, please?

47.1 「Another」

你可以在單數名詞前面或帶有數字的複數名詞前面使用 another。

Can I have another apple, please?

在單數名詞前面使用 another。

One 或不同的數字可以代替這個名詞。

Can I have another apple, please?

Can I have another one, please?

你可以用 one 這個詞或不同的數字來代替名詞。

用法

用 another 談論更多或不同版本的事物。

更多例子

I'd like **another two pears**, please.

I've finished my drink. Can I have **another one**, please?

Maria wants to borrow **another** book.

48「Both」

參見：
「Another」第 47 單元

48.1「Both」

I'm having both.

這意味着 Max 點了薯條和沙拉。

Both of them are having salad.

這意味着 Max 和 Andy 正在吃沙拉。

Both of the boys are having salad.

你可以在帶有 the、these 或 those 的複數名詞前面使用 both of。

用法

用 both 談論兩個人或事物。你可以單獨使用 both，或在兩個名詞、複數名詞前面使用，也可以在 we、us、they 或 them 後面使用。

用 both of 談論兩個人或事物。你可以在 us、you、them 前面使用 both of，或在帶有 the、these 或 those 的複數名詞前面使用。

更多例子

I like **both** jumpers.

They **both** love playing tennis.

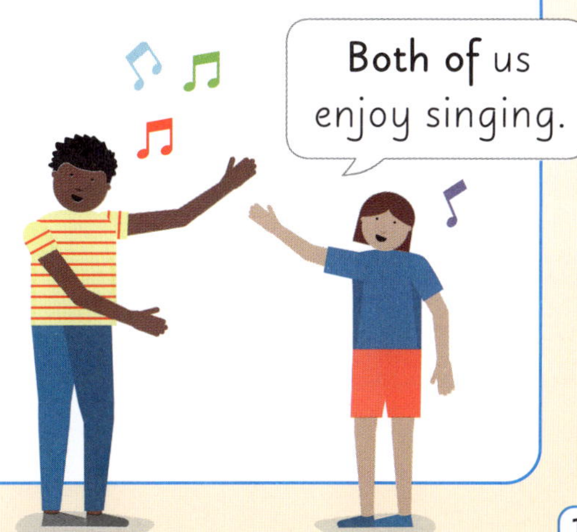

49「Each」和「every」

參見：
名詞 第 50 單元

49.1「Each」和「every」

通常 Each 和 every 意思相同。兩者在單數名詞前面使用。

I've tried	each / every	flavour.

在這個句子中，each 和 every 意思相同。

用法

用 each 和 every 整體描述一組事物。

更多例子

Each dog has a toy.

Every player is wearing a red T-shirt.

Each flower in the vase is pink.

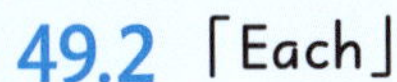

49.2 「Each」

有時 each 和 every 含義略有不同。

Andy filled **each** glass with juice.

用法

用 each 強調群體中的單個事物或少量事物。

49.3 「Every」

有時 every 和 each 含義略有不同。

I go swimming **every** Sunday.

用法

用 every 描述整體群體、大量事物，或談論日數、月份、季節或年份等時間。

更多例子

Each cat is a different colour.

Paint **each** shape blue.

更多例子

We go skiing **every** winter.

I've read **every** book on my bookshelf.

50 Nouns 名詞

參見：
冠詞 第 45 單元
數量 第 62 單元

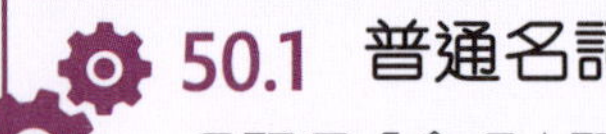

50.1 普通名詞

名詞是「命名」詞語。英文名詞沒有性別之分。
普通名詞指日常物件、動物、季節和動作。

house

baby

armchair

smile

farmer

spring

lunch

castle

giraffe

doll

50.2 專有名詞

專有名詞（proper nouns）指特定人物、地點、日子和月份，首字母必須大寫。

Mount Everest

Italy

Paris

Monday

November

Max

Maria

Texas

Lake Victoria

Central Park

50.3 單數與複數名詞

名詞分單數和複數。
單數名詞（singular noun）指一件事物。
複數名詞（plural noun）指兩件或以上事物，大多數名詞變複數時，只需在單數名詞後加 s。

在單數名詞後面加 s。

不規則複數名詞

以 x、z、ch 或 sh 結尾的名詞加 es。

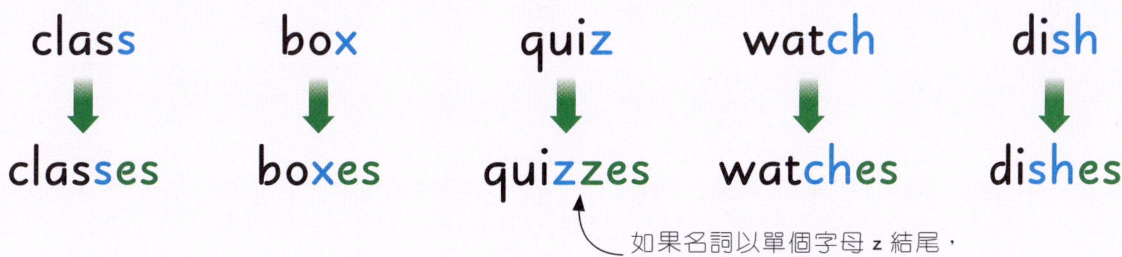

如果名詞以單個字母 z 結尾，則在加 es 之前再加一個 z。

大部分以字母 o 結尾的名詞，加 es 構成複數。如果 o 前面有其他母音字母，則只需加 s。

potato → potatoes

radio → radios

有些名詞完全不規則。請參閱 R26 不規則複數名詞列表。

child → children

person → people

對於子音字母加 y 結尾的名詞，要先將 y 變為 i，然後再加 es。

dictionary → dictionaries

story → stories

有些複數名詞保持不變。

fish → fish

sheep → sheep

50.4 可數和不可數名詞

可以逐個計數的名詞稱為可數名詞（countable nouns），不能計數的名詞稱為不可數名詞（uncountable nouns）。

可數名詞

可數名詞前面可以使用 a 、 an 、 some 、 any 或數字。

I need **a lemon** for the cake.

這是一個可數名詞，你可以數出有多少個檸檬。

I need **three lemons** for the cake.

這是一個可數名詞，你可以數出有多少個檸檬。

I need **some lemons** for the cake.

Some 表示檸檬的數量多於一個，但沒有具體說明。

Do we need **any lemons** for the cake?

在否定句和疑問句中，some 要變為 any。詳情請參閱 45.2 。

不可數名詞

不可數名詞前面可使用 some 或 any 。

I need **some flour** for the cake.

這是一個不可數名詞。你不能計數麵粉。

Is there **any flour** for the cake?

在否定句和疑問句中，some 變為 any 。詳情請參閱 45.2 。

50.5 「How many」和「How much」

詢問可數名詞的數量時，使用 how many 。

How many oranges do you need?

可數名詞使用 How many 。

詢問不可數名詞的數量時，使用 how much 。

How much rice is there?

不可數名詞使用 How much 。

更多例子

My dad bought **a car** today.

There's **some sand** in my shoe.

How many apples would you like?

How much sugar do we need?

51 Personal subject pronouns
人稱主格代詞

參見：
人稱賓格代詞 第 52 單元
反身代詞 第 53 單元

This is Maria. She likes books.

51.1 構成方法：人稱主格代詞

人稱主格代詞代替句子主語。

This is Maria. Maria likes books.

Maria 是句子主語。

This is Maria. She likes books.

She 是人稱主格代詞，代替 Maria 的名字。

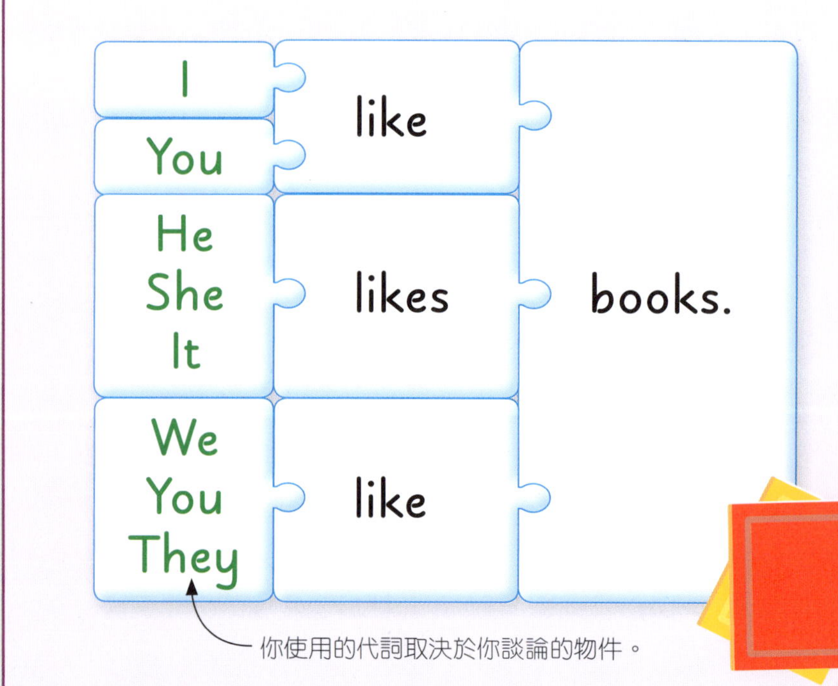

你使用的代詞取決於你談論的物件。

用法

用人稱主格代詞談論句子主語，常代替人名。

提示！

在英語中，you 的形式沒有禮貌或親昵的分別。無論你是在和一個人還是多個人交談，you 的形式都保持不變。

51.2 人稱主格代詞的用法

I'm ten years old today.

使用 I 指自己，首字母必須大寫。

You play the trumpet very well.

當你直接和他人交談時，使用 You。

He is in the playground.

使用 He 指男孩或男人。

She is doing her homework.

使用 She 指女孩或女人。

It has got a yellow ball.

使用 It 指物品或動物。

We are having fun at the beach.

使用 We 指包含自己在內的兩人以上群體。

You are happy!

當你直接和不止一個人交談時，使用 You。

They are playing baseball.

使用 They 指一群人、動物或物品。

52 Personal object pronouns
人稱賓格代詞

參見：
人稱主格代詞　第 51 單元
反身代詞　第 53 單元

The car is dirty, so we're washing it.

52.1 構成方法：人稱賓格代詞

人稱賓格代詞代替句子中的賓語。

The car is dirty, so we're washing **the car.**

The car is dirty, so we're washing **it.**

The car 是這個句子的賓語。

It 是一個人稱賓格代詞它代替了 the car。

用法

當你、他人或事物是句子賓語時，使用人稱賓格代詞，它們經常代替某個人的名字。

提示！
這個詞無論是指單獨一個人還是多個人，形式都是一樣的。

I	you	he	she	it	we	you	they	主格代詞
↓	↓	↓	↓	↓	↓	↓	↓	
me	you	him	her	it	us	you	them	賓格代詞

52.2 人稱賓格代詞的用法

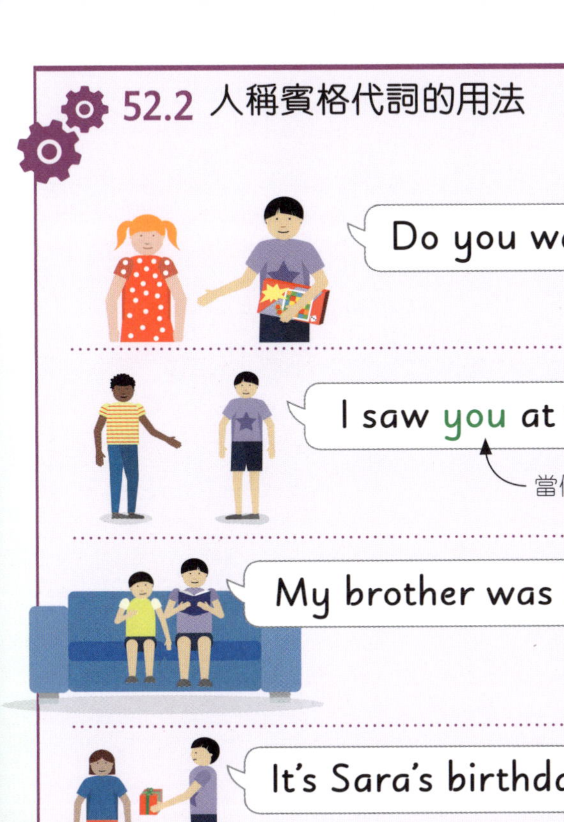

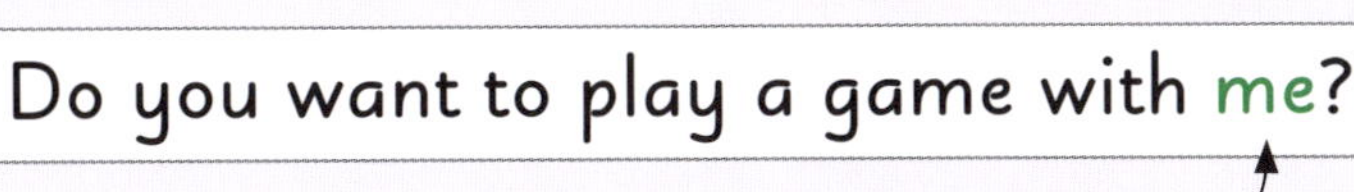

Do you want to play a game with **me**?

使用 me 指自己。

I saw **you** at the park yesterday.

當你直接和某個人說話時，用 you。

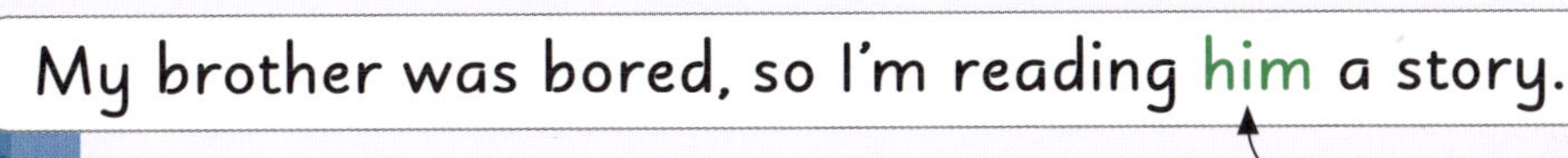

My brother was bored, so I'm reading **him** a story.

使用 him 指男孩或男人。

It's Sara's birthday, so I am giving **her** a present.

使用 her 指女孩或女人。

Mia lost her pencil and I found **it**.

使用 it 指物品或動物。

Dad gave **us** some money.

使用 us 指包含自己的兩人以上群體。

Can I take a picture of **you**?

當你直接和多於一個說話時，使用 you。

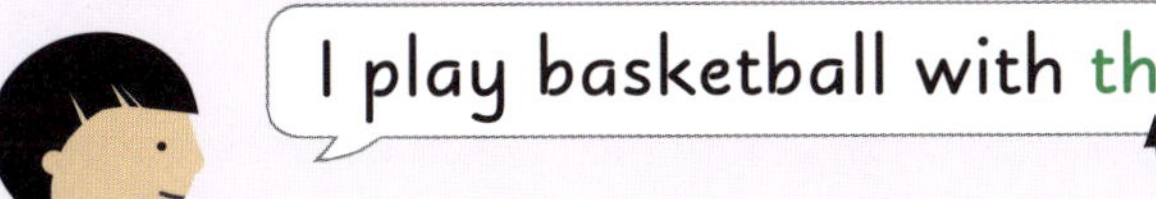

I play basketball with **them**.

使用 them 指一群人、動物或物品。

53 Reflexive pronouns
反身代詞

參見：
人稱主格代詞 第 51 單元
人稱賓格代詞 第 52 單元

53.1 構成方法：反身代詞

英文中的反身代詞以 self 或 selves 結尾。

這是一個反身代詞。

用法

反身代詞用於句子的主語和賓語是相同的人物、群體、事物或多個事物。

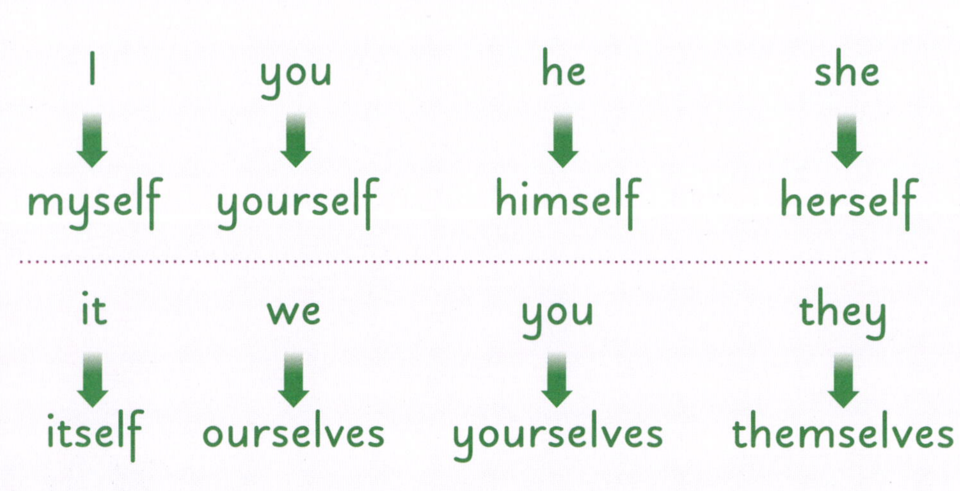

提示！

使用反身代詞時，單數 you (yourself) 和複數 you (yourselves) 有區別。

53.2 反身代詞的用法

I bought myself a new toy with my birthday money.
當主語是 I 時，用 myself。
Oh no! You've hurt yourself.
當主語是指一個人的 You 時，使用 yourself。
Andy is teaching himself the guitar.
當主語是 He 或一個男孩、男人的名字時，使用 himself。
She has made herself a sandwich.
當主語是 She 或一個女孩、女人的名字時，使用 herself。
Look at the cat. It's licking itself.
當主語是 It 時，使用 itself。
We are taking a picture of ourselves.
當主語是 We 時，使用 ourselves。
Can you see yourselves in the mirror?
當主語是指多於一個人的 you 時，使用 yourselves。
They are enjoying themselves.
當主語是 They 或不止一個人的名字時，使用 themselve。

54 Indefinite pronouns 不定代詞

不定代詞是我們談論不特定人物或事物的詞。

54.1「Someone」

在肯定句或疑問句中，用 **someone** 談論不特定的人。

54.2「Anyone」

在否定句中用 **anyone** 表示沒有人，或在肯定句、疑問句中談論不特定的人。

更多例子

Someone phoned when we were eating dinner.

Is **someone** knocking at the door?

I saw **someone** I know at the park.

更多例子

There isn't **anyone** on the stage.

Does **anyone** want to play tennis with me?

Does **anyone** want some juice?

參見：
構成疑問句 第 38 單元

54.3 「Everyone」

在肯定句或疑問句中，用 everyone 談論一群人。

54.4 「No one」

在肯定句中用 no one 表示沒有人。

更多例子

I invited **everyone** in my class to my birthday party.

The teacher asked **everyone** to be quiet.

Is **everyone** having fun?

更多例子

There was **no one** at the bus stop.

No one knew the answer to the question.

There's **no one** in the garden.

54.5 「Something」

在肯定句或疑問句中，用 something 談論未指明或未命名的事物。

54.6 「Anything」

在肯定句、否定句或疑問句中，用 anything 談論未指明或未命名的事物。

更多例子

Sofia can see **something** in the box. What is it?

There's **something** in this bag. It's a surprise!

更多例子

Ben is a great artist. He can draw **anything**.

It's so dark. I can't see **anything**!

Would you like **anything** to drink?

54.7 「Everything」

在肯定句、否定句或疑問句中，用 everything 談論整組事物。

54.8 「Nothing」

當東西不存在時，肯定句中用 nothing，而在否定句和大部分疑問句中，改用 anything。

更多例子

Andy likes **everything** in this toyshop.

Have we got **everything** we need to bake a cake?

更多例子

My room is really tidy. There's **nothing** on the floor!

I'm bored. There's **nothing** to do!

There's **nothing** in this bag. It's empty.

55 Possessive adjectives
所有格形容詞

參見：
所有格代詞 第 56 單元
所有格撇號 第 57 單元

Poppy is my cat.

George is her cat.

55.1 所有格形容詞

在名詞前面使用所有格形容詞，形式根據所有者是單數、複數、男性或女性而發生變化。

主語 + 動詞	所有格形容詞	名詞
Poppy is	my	cat.

這代表這隻貓屬於我。

your 沒有禮貌或親暱形式。無論你和一個人還是多於一個人交談，your 的形式都保持不變。

用法

在名詞前面使用所有格形容詞表明其所屬對象，或在家庭成員前面使用。使用的所有格形容詞取決於所有者是誰，而不是取決於該名詞。

55.2 所有格形容詞的用法

This is my brother, Tom.

使用 my 指屬於自己的事物。

Here are your presents, Ben!

使用 your 指正在交談對象的事物。

It's his birthday today.

使用 his 指屬於男孩或男人的事物。

This is her bag.

使用 her 指屬於女孩或女人的事物。

The dog is playing with its ball.

使用 its 指屬於動物或物品的事物。

This is our new computer.

使用 our 指包括自己在內至少兩人群體的事物。

Is this your puppy?

使用 your 指正在交談話對象的事物。

They are playing with their toys.

使用 their 指屬於一群人的事物。

56 Possessive pronouns

所有格代詞

參見：
所有格形容詞 第 55 單元
所有格撇號 第 57 單元

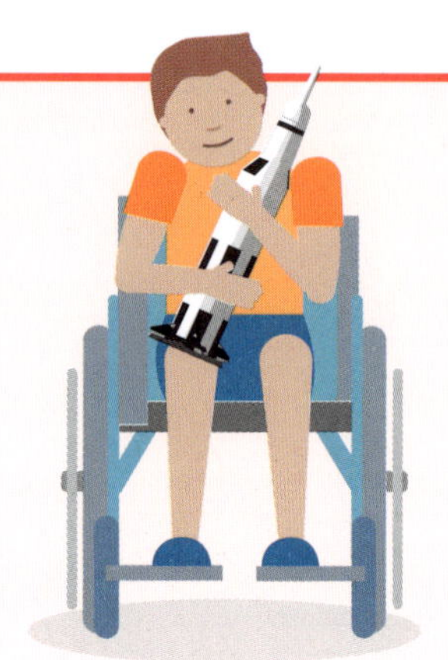

56.1 構成方法：所有格代詞

所有格代詞用來代替單數或複數名詞，並表示所屬關係。

This rocket is my rocket.

This rocket is mine.

mine 代替 my rocket。

This rocket is mine.

This rocket is yours.

This rocket is his.

This rocket is hers.

This rocket is ours.

This rocket is yours.

This rocket is theirs.

yours 沒有禮貌或親暱形式。無論你是在和一個人還是多個人交談，yours 的形式都相同。

用法

用所有格代詞談論人物擁有的東西。選擇哪個代詞取決於所有者是誰，而不是該名詞是甚麼，it 沒有對應的所有格代詞。

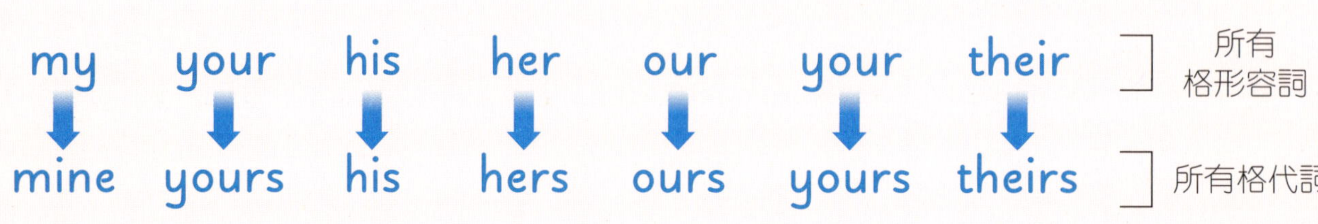

56.2 所有格代詞的用法

Your robot is bigger than **mine**.

使用 mine 指屬於你的東西。

Is this kite **yours**?

使用 yours 指屬於你正在交談的人的東西。

That burger is **his**.

使用 his 指屬於男孩或男人的東西。

My dress is green and **hers** is red.

使用 hers 指屬於女孩或女人的東西。

These toys are **ours**.

使用 ours 指屬於至少包括你自己在內的兩個人的群體的東西。

Is that cat **yours**?

使用 yours 指屬於你們正在對話的人的東西。

That house is **theirs**.

使用 theirs 指屬於兩個或更多人的東西。

57 Possessive apostrophes

所有格撇號（'s）

57.1 構成方法：所有格撇號（'s）

表示人物或事物所擁有的事物時，在名詞或人名後面加's，有時只需加'。

That is the house of Ben.

That is Ben's house.

大多數人名或單數名詞，加's。

James's house

James' house

以 s 結尾的人名或單數名詞，加's 或加'。

用法

使用所有格撇號表示所屬關係。

My grandparents' house

以 s 結尾的複數名詞，只需加'。

The children's house

不以 s 結尾的複數名詞，加's。

參見：
所有格形容詞 第 55 單元
所有格代詞 第 56 單元

更多例子：

This is Maria**'s** cat.

Thomas**'s** dog is small.

The doll**'s** dress is pink.

Chris**'** hair is black.

Amy**'s** dad is very tall.

The men**'s** T-shirts are green.

Have you seen Andy**'s** bag?

This is my parents**'** car.

58 Relative pronouns

關係代詞

參見：
分句 第 R6 小節

使用關係代詞 who 、 that 、 which 和 where 來引導關係分句。關係分句提供更多關於主句中所提及事物的資訊。

58.1 「who」和「that」

This is my friend. He likes robots.

關係代詞

This is my friend [who / that] likes robots.

主句　　關係分句

用法

使用 who 或 that 引導關於人的關係分句。

58.2 「which」和「that」

Ben drew a picture. It was very nice.

關係代詞

Ben drew a picture [which / that] was very nice.

主句　　關係分句

用法

使用 which 或 that 引導關於事物的關係分句。

58.3 「where」

This is the field. We play baseball here.

關係代詞

This is the field [where] we play baseball.

主句　　關係分句

用法

使用 where 引導關於地點的關係分句。

It's my brother **that** plays football, not me.

更多例子

I've got a sister **who** is a doctor.

This is my cousin **who** speaks English.

I bought a new toy **which** I love.

This is the present **that** Andy gave me.

She read a book **that** was really interesting.

The street **where** I live is called Main Street.

This is the cafe **where** we met Sofia.

This is the pool **where** they swim on Saturdays.

59 「There is」和「there are」

參見：
名詞 第 50 單元
「There was」和「there were」第 60 單元

59.1 構成方法：「there is」和「there are」

在單數和不可數名詞前面使用 there is 或 there's 。

There	is	單數名詞和不可數名詞
There	is	one giraffe.

用 There is 或 There are 談論當前存在的一個或多個事物。

There's

我們經常將 There is 縮寫為 There's 。

用法

There is 或 there are 用來談論當前存在的某一事物或多個事物。

在複數名詞前面使用 there are 。

There	are	複數名詞
There	are	two elephants.

用 There are 談論多於一個事物。

There's one giraffe.

There are two elephants.

更多例子

There's a kite.

There is one orange flower.

There are eight stars in the sky.

There are some cows in the field.

There's a bag on the floor.

There is some rice on my plate.

There are two ants.

There's some fruit in the bowl.

There are four cars.

59.2 構成方法：「there is」和「there are」否定句

構成 there is 和 there are 否定句，需在 is 或 are 後面加 not。在單數名詞或不可數名詞前面使用 there is not。

There is a hippo.

There is not a hippo.

There isn't a hippo.

用法

使用 there is 或 there are 否定句談論當前時刻不存在的某一或多個事物。

在複數名詞前面使用 there are not

There are some lions.

There are not any lions.

There aren't any lions.

some 變成 any。前往 45.2 了解更多資訊。

更多例子

There isn't any honey left.

There aren't any people in the cinema.

There isn't any food in the cupboard.

59.3 構成方法：「there is」和「there are」疑問句

構成 there is 和 there are 疑問句，需將 is 或 are 放在 there 前面。
在單數名詞或不可數名詞前面使用 is there 。

There is a crocodile.

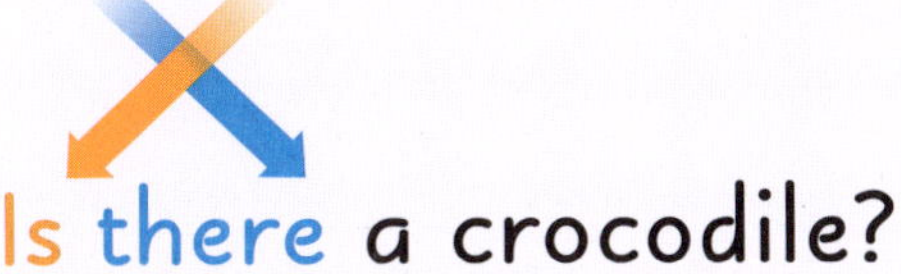

Is there a crocodile?

將 Is 放在 there 前面。

在複數名詞前面使用 are there 。

There are some lizards.

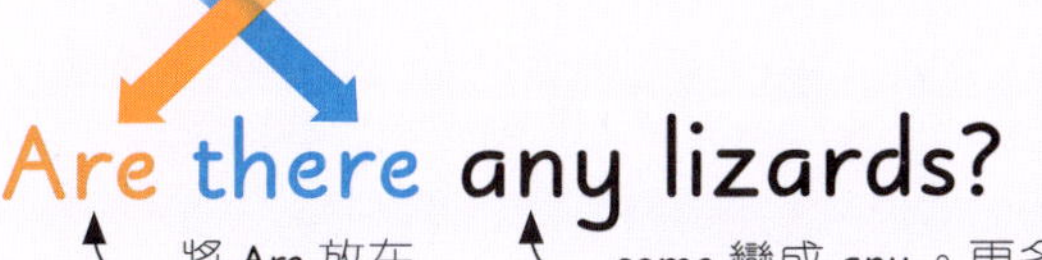

Are there any lizards?

將 Are 放在 there 前面。

some 變成 any 。更多內容請參閱 45.2 。

用法

使用 there is 或 there are 疑問句詢問當前時刻是否存在一個或多個事物。

更多例子

Is there a train station in your town?

Are there any toys in your room?

Is there any milk in the jug?

60 「There was」和「there were」

參見：
名詞 第 50 單元
「There is」和「there are」第 59 單元

There was a clown at the party.

There were balloons.

60.1 構成方法：「there was」和「there were」

在單數名詞或不可數名詞前面使用 there was 。

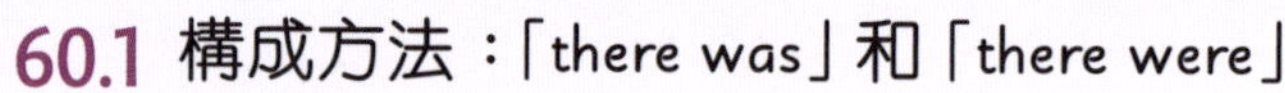

There	was	單數名詞或不可數名詞
There	was	a clown.

用 There was 談論一個事物或不可數名詞。

在複數名詞前面使用 there were 。

There	were	複數名詞
There	were	balloons.

用 There were 談論多於一個的事物。

用法

用 there was 或 there were 談論過去存在的一個或多個事物。

更多例子

There were two giraffes.

There were lots of books in the library.

There was one biscuit in the jar.

There was a bird in the tree.

There was some chocolate on the table.

There was a competition at school today.

There were three ducks in the water.

There were dolphins in the sea.

There were some children at the park.

60.2 構成方法：「there was」和「there were」否定句

構成 there was 和 there were 否定句，在 was 或 were 後面加 not。
在單數名詞或不可數名詞前面使用 there was not。

There was a cake at the party.

There was not a cake at the party.

There wasn't a cake at the party.

在複數名詞前面使用 there were not。

There were some games at the party.

There were not any games at the party.

There weren't any games at the party.

some 變為 any。詳情請參閱 45.2。

用法

用 there was 或 there were 否定句談論過去不存在的一個或多個事物。

更多例子

There weren't any teddy bears in the toyshop.

There wasn't a lift, so I used the stairs.

There wasn't any grass in the garden.

60.3 構成方法：「there was」和「there were」疑問句

構成 there was 和 there were 疑問句，需將 was 或 were 放在 there 前面。
在單數名詞或不可數名詞前面使用 was there 。

There was music.

Was there music?

將 Was 放在 there 前面。

用法

使用 there was 或 there were 疑問句詢問過去是否存在一個或多個事物。

在複數名詞前面使用 were there 。

There were presents.

Were there presents?

將 Were 放在 there 前面。

更多例子

Was there a swimming pool at your hotel?

Were there lots of people at the beach?

Was there any juice at the shop?

61 Numbers 數字

我們用數字來計數和說明事物的數量。

參見：
數量 第 62 單元
音節 第 R4 小節

61.1 數字

0 zero	1 one	2 two	3 three	4 four	5 five
6 six	7 seven	8 eight	9 nine	10 ten	11 eleven
12 twelve	13 thirteen	14 fourteen	15 fifteen	16 sixteen	17 seventeen
18 eighteen	19 nineteen	20 twenty	21 twenty-one	22 twenty-two	23 twenty-three
24 twenty-four	25 twenty-five	26 twenty-six	27 twenty-seven	28 twenty-eight	29 twenty-nine
30 thirty	40 forty	50 fifty	60 sixty	70 seventy	80 eighty
90 ninety	100 one hundred	101 one hundred and one	200 two hundred	300 three hundred	400 four hundred
500 five hundred	600 six hundred	700 seven hundred	800 eight hundred	900 nine hundred	1000 one thousand

61.2 發音相似的數字：

這些數字的發音非常相似，確保你讀的音節是正確的重音，以免混淆。

13	thir<u>teen</u>	30	<u>thir</u>ty
14	four<u>teen</u>	40	<u>for</u>ty
15	fif<u>teen</u>	50	<u>fif</u>ty
16	six<u>teen</u>	60	<u>six</u>ty
17	seven<u>teen</u>	70	<u>seven</u>ty
18	eigh<u>teen</u>	80	<u>eigh</u>ty
19	nine<u>teen</u>	90	<u>nine</u>ty

最後的音節發重音。

開首音節發重音。

61.3 序數（ordinal numbers）

我們用序數表示事物在列表中的位置。

1st first	2nd second	3rd third	4th fourth	5th fifth	6th sixth	7th seventh

8th eighth	9th ninth	10th tenth	11th eleventh	12th twelfth	13th thirteenth
14th fourteenth	15th fifteenth	16th sixteenth	17th seventeenth	18th eighteenth	19th nineteenth
20th twentieth	21st twenty-first	22nd twenty-second	23rd twenty-third	24th twenty-fourth	25th twenty-fifth
26th twenty-sixth	27th twenty-seventh	28th twenty-eighth	29th twenty-ninth	30th thirtieth	31st thirty-first

62 Quantity 數量

英語中有幾個詞可以用來描述事物的數量。

參見：
冠詞 第 45 單元
名詞 第 50 單元

62.1 數量詞

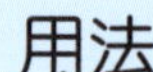

There are **some** houses near the cafe.

用法

在複數名詞或不可數名詞前使用 some，表示不確定數量或分量的事物。

There are **a few** ducks in the pond.

在複數名詞前使用 a few 談論少量的事物。

I saw **lots of** butterflies in the garden.

在複數名詞或不可數名詞前使用 lots of 或 a lot of，談論大量的事物或數量。

There's **enough** flour to make this cake.

當你擁有所需數量或分量的事物時，在複數名詞或不可數名詞前使用 enough。

There are **too many** lemons!

當你擁有的事物超過所需數量時，在複數名詞前使用 too many。

There's **too much** sugar in the bowl.

當你擁有的事物超過所需數量時，在不可數名詞前使用 too much。

There's **a little** honey, but we need more.

當有少量事物時，在不可數名詞前使用 a little 或 a little bit of。

更多例子

There are **some** stars in the sky.

A few children were late to school today.

There are **lots of** birds in the garden.

I painted **a lot of** pictures today.

We have got **enough** apples for the picnic.

There are **too many** toys on the floor.

I have got **too much** rice in my bowl.

Can I have **a little bit of** cake, please?

There's **a little** milk left.

63 Adjectives 形容詞

參見：
名詞　第 50 單元
強調詞　第 71 單元

63.1 形容詞的用法

a **dirty** dog

a **wet** dog

a **big** dog

a **small** dog

63.2 構成方法：形容詞

在英語中，形容詞通常放在名詞前面。描述單數名詞和複數名詞時，形容詞形式保持不變。

形容詞放在名詞前面。

句子開頭	形容詞	複數名詞
They are	small	dogs.

形容詞用於複數名詞時形式保持不變。

用法

用形容詞描述名詞。

當形容詞跟在某些動詞後面時，例如 to be，它們可以放在名詞後面。

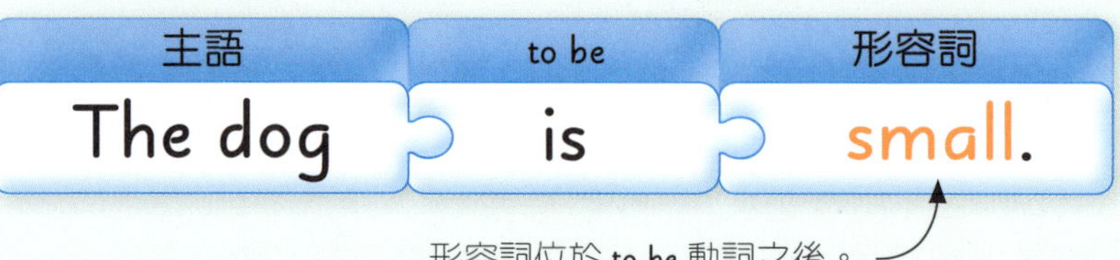

形容詞位於 to be 動詞之後。

更多例子

I love **funny** films.

I have got a **new** robot.

The clown was very **silly**.

I like your **blue** bag.

Andy's wearing a **purple** T-shirt.

My dogs are **friendly**.

提示！

你可以在形容詞前面使用 **very** 或 **really** 加強語氣。前往 71.1 了解更多資訊。

We're really **happy**.

It's very **windy** today.

64 Comparative adjectives 比較級形容詞

64.1 構成方法：比較級形容詞

大多數單音節形容詞和部分雙音節形容詞，在形容詞後加 er 構成比較級。

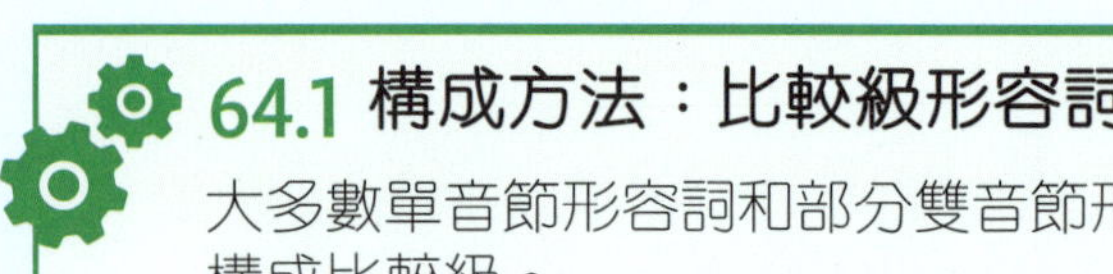

如果你要把事物與另一事物進行比較，在比較級形容詞後使用 than。

用法

使用比較級形容詞比較兩個或多個事物。

64.2 拼寫規則：比較級形容詞

構成這些比較級形容詞，需在形容詞後加 er。有時，在加 er 之前，形容詞的拼寫會發生變化。

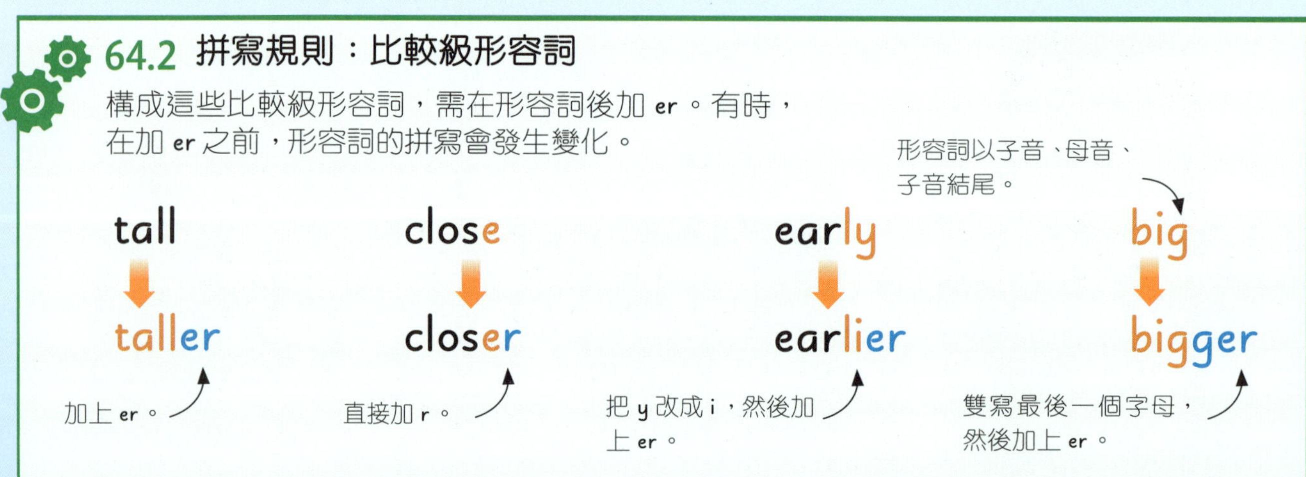

參見：
形容詞　第 63 單元
音節　第 R4 小節

64.3 構成方法：不規則比較級形容詞

Good 和 bad 有不規則的比較級形容詞形式。

good　　bad　　形容詞

better　　worse　　比較級形容詞

更多例子

The tree is **bigger than** the flower.

Our cat is much **lazier than** our dog.

The weather was bad yesterday, but today it's **worse**.

提示！
你可以在比較級形容詞前面加 **much** 加強語氣。更多內容請查看 71.2。

My bike is much **cleaner** than yours.

I'm quite good at the violin, and I'm getting **better**.

64.4 構成方法：長形容詞比較級

大部分雙音節形容詞和所有三音節或以上的形容詞，在形容詞前面加 more，不加 er。在任何形容詞前面加 less，可表達與 more 相反的意思。

形容詞比較級

主語 + 動詞	more/less	形容詞	than	句子其他部分
The rocket is	more less	expensive	than	the robot.

更多例子

I think board games are **more exciting than** video games.

The red flower is beautiful, but the purple flower is **more beautiful.**

This puzzle is **less difficult than** that puzzle.

提示！

音節是單詞的一部分。單詞中的每個母音音素就是一個音節。更多內容請查閱 R4。

The pizzas were **more delicious than** the sandwiches.

The purple snake is **more colourful than** the green snake.

65 Superlative adjectives
最高級形容詞

參見：
形容詞 第 63 單元
音節 第 R4 小節

I am tall. Sofia is taller than me. Max is the tallest.

65.1 構成方法：最高級形容詞

對於大多數單音節形容詞和部分雙音節形容詞，構成最高級形容詞時，需在形容詞後面加 est。

主語	動詞	the	最高級形容詞
I	am	the	tallest.

在最高級形容詞前加冠詞 the。

在形容詞 tall 後加 est 構成最高級形式。

用法

用最高級形容詞來談論極端情況。

65.2 拼寫規則：最高級形容詞

構成這些最高級形容詞，需在形容詞後面加 est。有時，在加 est 之前，形容詞的拼寫會有一點變化。

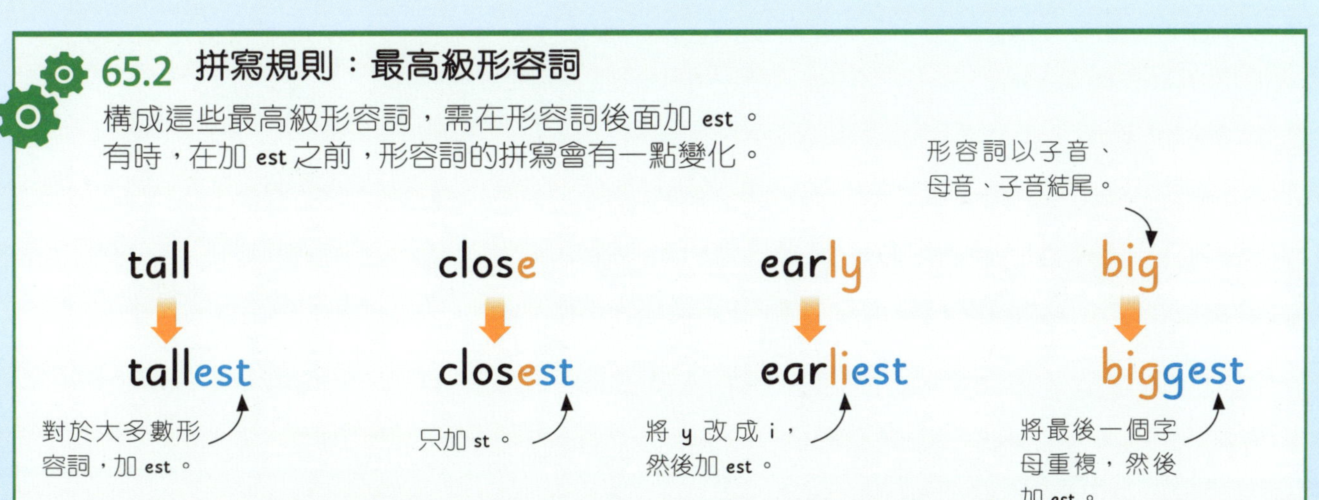

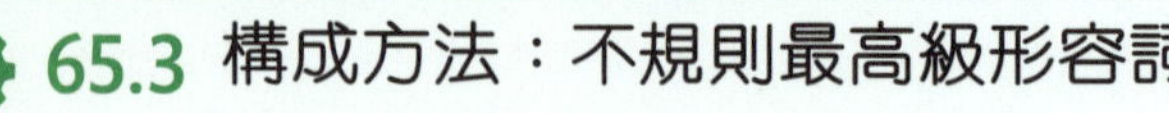

65.3 構成方法：不規則最高級形容詞

Good 和 bad 有不規則的最高級形容詞形式。

good	bad	形容詞
better	worse	比較級形容詞
best	worst	最高級形容詞

更多例子

Today was **the coldest** day of the year.

The closest park is five minutes from my house.

The black and white dog is **the biggest**.

This is **the worst** cake I've ever tasted.

Saturday was **the sunniest** day this week.

Jess is my **best** friend.

65.4 構成方法：長形容詞最高級

大部分雙音節形容詞和所有三音節及以上的形容詞，需在形容詞前面加 the most，不加 est。在任何形容詞前面加 the least，可表達與 the most 相反的意思。

主語 + 動詞	the	most/least	形容詞
Sara is	the	most least	excited.

最高級形容詞：most/least + 形容詞

更多例子

I think maths is **the most important** subject at school.

This is **the most interesting** museum in our city.

He is **the least afraid** of spiders.

The Eiffel Tower is **the most famous** landmark in Paris.

That's **the most amazing** rainbow I've ever seen!

提示！

音節是單詞的一部分。單詞中的每個母音發音都是一個音節。前往 R4 查閱更多資訊。

66 Adverbs of manner
情態副詞

參見：
形容詞 第 63 單元
強調詞 第 71 單元

66.1 構成方法：情態副詞

大部分情態副詞是在形容詞後面加 ly 。副詞位於其所修飾的動詞後面。
如果動詞帶有賓語，副詞則位於賓語後面。

大部分情態副詞以 ly 結尾。

用法

使用情態副詞描述動詞，說明人物或事物如何做事情。

66.2 拼寫規則：情態副詞

大部分情態副詞是在形容詞後面加 ly 。
有時在加 ly 前，形容詞的拼寫會發現一些變化。

形容詞以字母 y 結尾。

形容詞以子音字母加 le 結尾。

大部分副詞，加 ly 。

將 y 改成 i ，然後加 ly 。

不要 e ，然後加 ly 。

66.3 構成方法：不規則情態副詞

有些情態副詞是不規則的。副詞 **well** 看起來不像它對應的形容詞 **good**。有些副詞與其形容詞形式相同。以下是一些常見的不規則情態副詞。

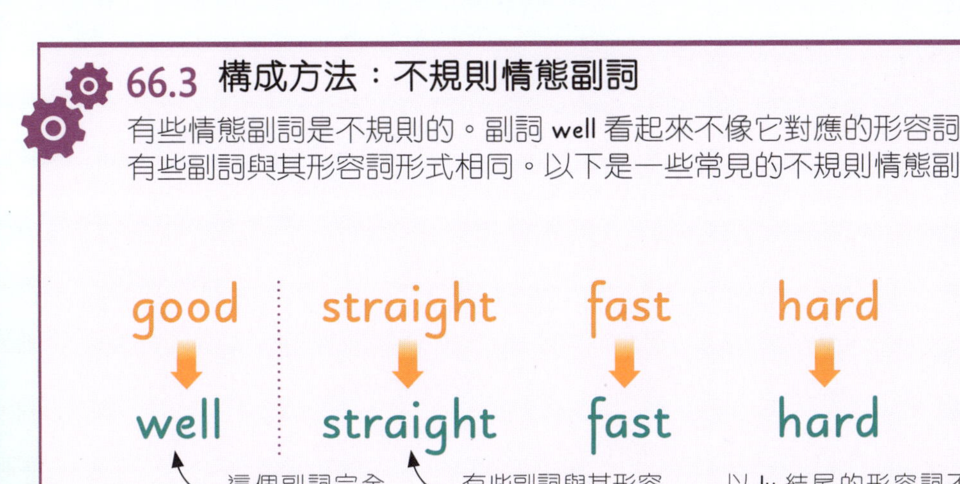

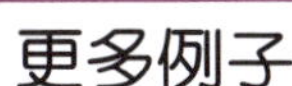

更多例子

The car is moving really **fast**.

Sara stroked the cat **gently**.

She sings **beautifully**.

Ben can play the piano very **well**.

Maria had to get up **early** today.

注意！

在情態副詞前面使用 very 或 really 以加強程度。前往 71.1 了解更多資訊。

67 Comparative adverbs

比較級副詞

參見：
比較級形容詞　第 64 單元
情態副詞　第 66 單元

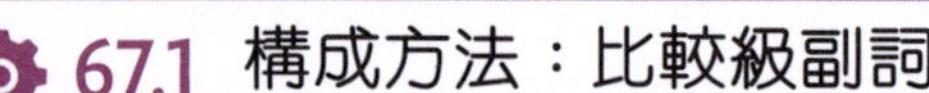

I run quickly, but Sofia runs more quickly.

67.1 構成方法：比較級副詞

大部分比較級副詞的構成是在副詞前面加 more 或 less。當某人做事情的程度比他人更高時用 more，less 則表示相反的意思。

比較級副詞

主語	動詞	more/less	副詞
Sofia	runs	more less	quickly.

在副詞前面加 more 或 less。

這個副詞保持不變。

當與其他事物進行比較時，在比較級副詞後面使用 than。

主語	動詞	more/less	副詞	than	句子其他部分
Sofia	runs	more less	quickly	than	Max.

在比較級副詞後面使用 than。

用法

使用比較級副詞比較兩個或更多人或物做事情的方式。

記住！

你可以在比較級副詞前面加 much 來加強語氣。前往 71.2 了解更多資訊。

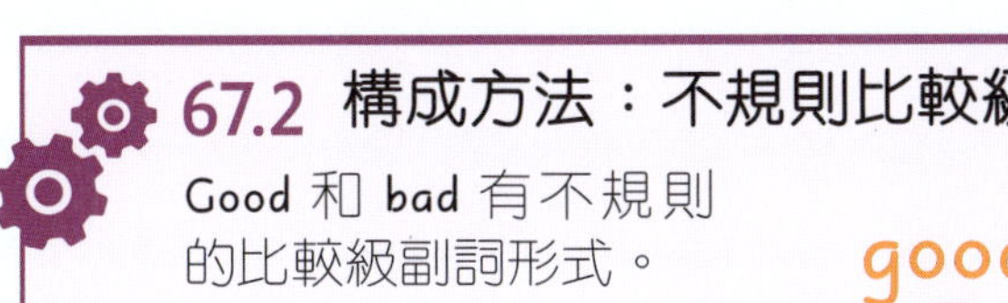

67.2 構成方法：不規則比較級副詞

Good 和 bad 有不規則的比較級副詞形式。

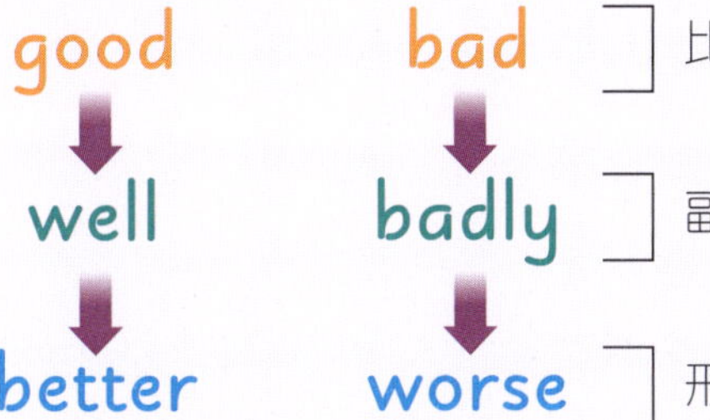

	good	bad
比較級副詞	good	bad
副詞	well	badly
形容詞	better	worse

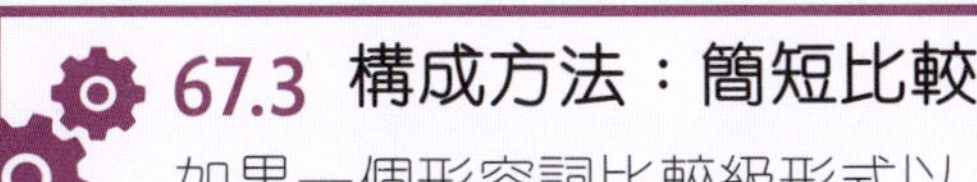

67.3 構成方法：簡短比較級副詞

如果一個形容詞比較級形式以 **er** 結尾，你可以用這個形式來代替 **more** 加副詞。

主語 + 動詞	比較級副詞	句子其他部分
Sofia runs	more quickly	than Max.
	quicker	

這裏 **more quickly** 和 **quicker** 意思相同。

記住！
要了解更多關於比較級形容詞的內容，請參閱第 64 單元。

更多例子

Andy speaks **louder than** Sofia.

Sara paints **more carefully than** me.

Maria plays the violin much **better than** Ben.

This cheese smells **worse than** that cheese.

68 Superlative adverbs
最高級副詞

參見：
最高級形容詞 第 65 單元
情態副詞 第 66 單元

68.1 構成方法：最高級副詞

構成大多數最高級副詞，需在副詞前面加上 the most 或 the least。

最高級副詞

主語	動詞	the	moss/least	副詞
Sofia	runs	the	most least	quickly.

在 most 或 least 前面加上 the。

副詞保持不變。

用法

用最高級副詞描述做事情的極端情程。

當某人做事情比其他人多時，使用 the most。
當某人做事情比其他人少時，使用 the least。

Sofia runs the most quickly.

Andy runs the least quickly.

The least 表示 the most 的相反意義。

68.2 構成方法：不規則最高級副詞

Good 和 bad 有不規則的最高級副詞形式。

good	bad	形容詞
well	badly	副詞
better	worse	比較級副詞
best	worst	最高級副詞

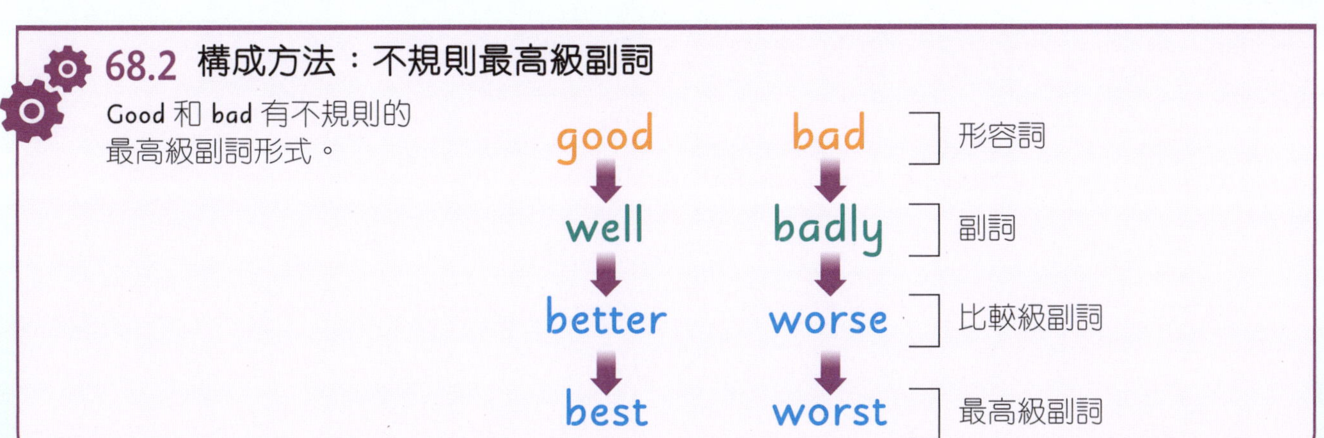

68.3 構成方法：簡短最高級副詞

如果形容詞最高級形式以 est 結尾，你可以用這個形式代替 the most + 副詞結構。

主語 + 動詞	最高級副詞
Sofia runs	the most quickly.
	the quickest.

這裏 the most quickly 和 the quickest 意思相同。

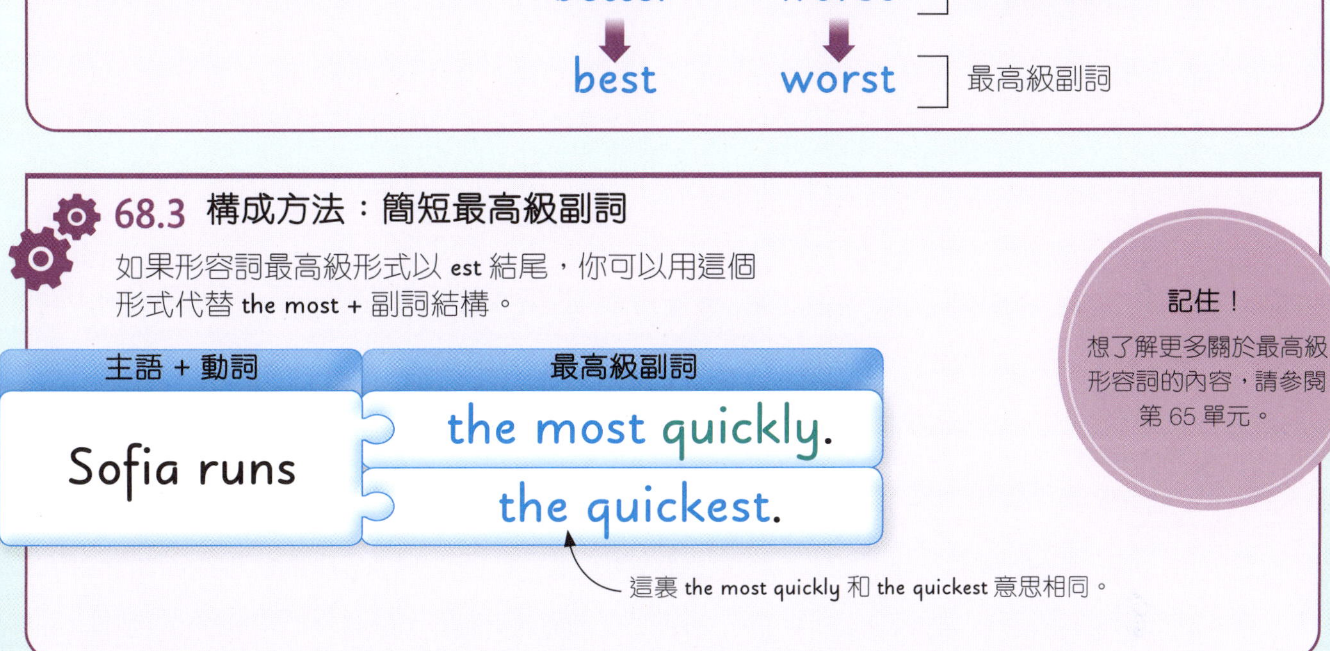

記住！

想了解更多關於最高級形容詞的內容，請參閱第 65 單元。

更多例子

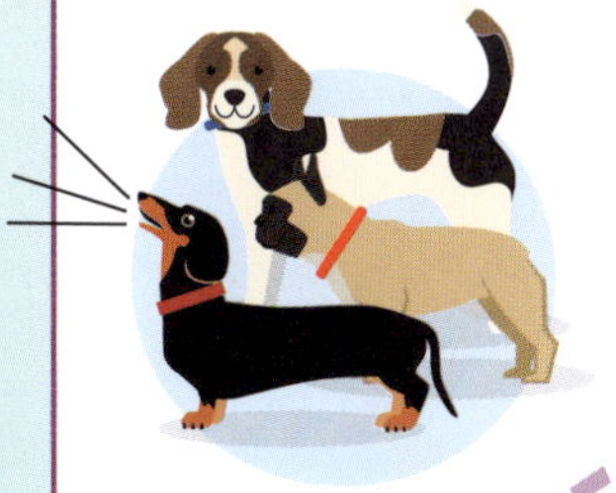

The black dog barks the most loudly.

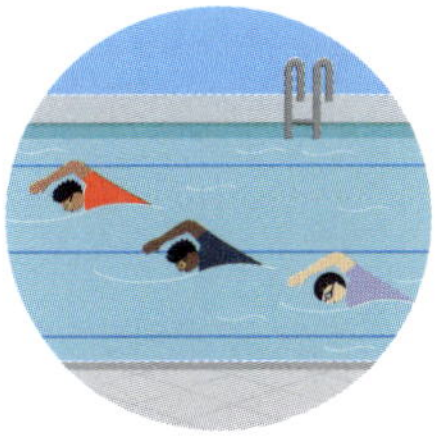

Max swims the fastest.

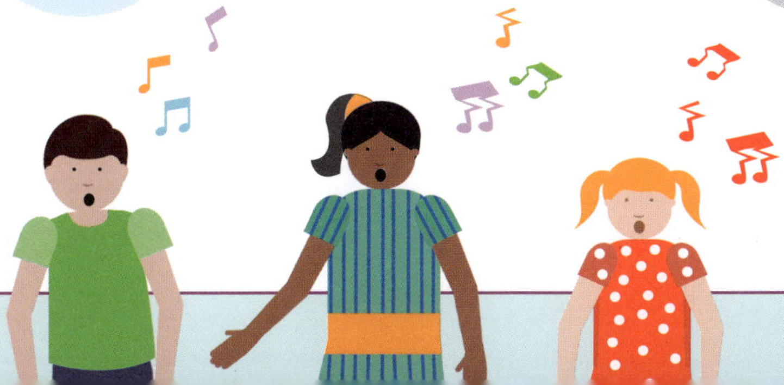

Maria sings the least beautifully.

69 Adverbs of time 時間副詞

參見：
頻率副詞 第 70 單元
時間介詞 第 74 單元

使用時間副詞談論現在正在進行的動作，或明確說明事情在現在發生、過去發生或將來會發生的時間。

69.1「now」

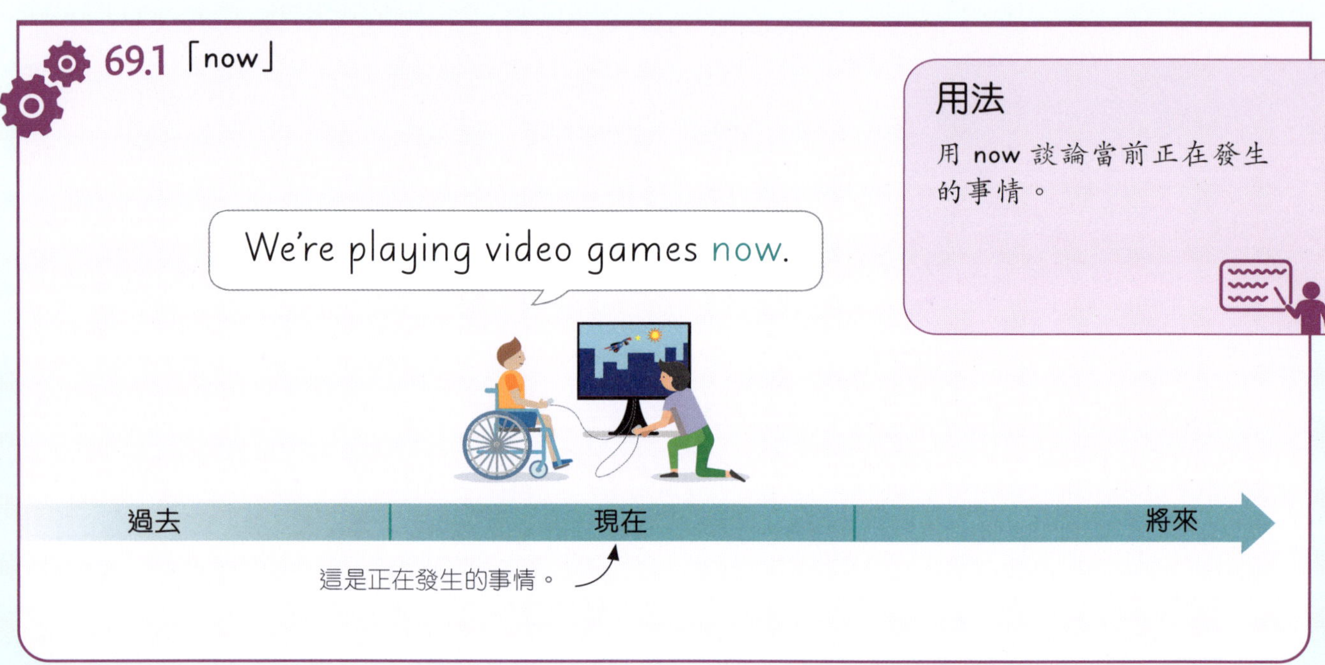

用法

用 now 談論當前正在發生的事情。

We're playing video games now.

過去　現在　將來

這是正在發生的事情。

69.2「still」

用法

用 still 談論過去開始並持續到現在的動作或狀態。

I am still painting my picture.

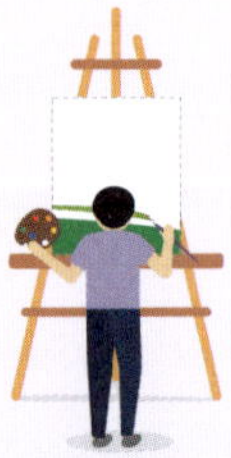

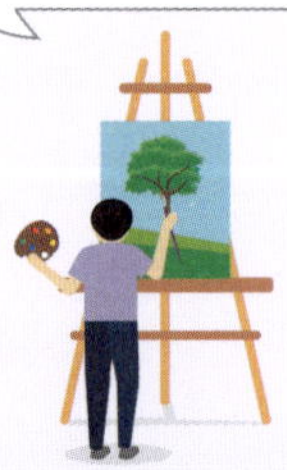

過去　現在　將來

Andy 在過去某個時候開始畫畫。

Andy 現在還在繼續畫畫。

69.3「about to」

用法

用 about to 談論即將在極近的將來發生的事情。

69.4「soon」

用法

用 soon 談論即將在不久的將來發生的事情。

69.5「yet」

用法

在否定句和疑問句中使用 yet 談論尚未發生但將來會發生的事情。

69.6「just」

用法

用 just 談論剛才在極近的過去發生的事情。

69.7「already」

用法

用 already 談論過去已經發生的事情，有時指事情比預期更早發生。

69.8「ago」

用法

將 ago 與分鐘、小時、天、月或年等時間標記連用，談論自過去某件事發生以來已經過去了多長時間。

更多例子

now	用於談論當前正在發生的事情。	What are you doing **now**? Sorry, we have got to go **now**.
still	用於談論過去開始並持續至今的動作或狀態。	They're **still** running the race. It's **still** raining.
about to	用於談論即將在極近的將來發生的事情。	We're **about to** go shopping. I'm **about to** play ice hockey.
soon	用於談論即將在不久的將來發生的事情。	Dinner will be ready **soon**. Get ready to go, we're leaving **soon**.
yet	用於談論尚未發生，但將來會發生的事情。	Has Andy woken up **yet**? I haven't finished my drawing **yet**.
just	用於談論剛才在極近的過去發生的事情。	I've **just** washed the dishes. We've **just** arrived in Miami.
already	用於談論已經發生的事情，有時指比預期更早發生。	I've **already** done my homework. The film has **already** started.
ago	用於談論事情發生後面過去了多長時間。	I took this photo three days **ago**. A week **ago**, we were in Australia.

70 Adverbs of frequency

頻率副詞

參見：
時間副詞 第 69 單元
時間介詞 第 74 單元

70.1 頻率副詞的用法

用頻率副詞談論事情發生的頻率。

100% → 0%		用法
I **always** brush my teeth in the morning.		當事情一直發生時，使用 always。
I **usually** get up at 7 o'clock.		當事情有規律地發生，但並非一直發生時，使用 usually。
I **often** have toast for breakfast.		當事情頻繁發生時，使用 often。
I **sometimes** play football on Sundays.		當事情偶然發生時，使用 sometimes。
I **never** walk to school. It's too far away.		當事情完全不會發生時，使用 never。

70.2 構成方法：頻率副詞

頻率副詞通常放在動詞前面。

主語	頻率副詞	動詞	句子其他部分
I	always	read	a book in the evening.

頻率副詞放在動詞前面。

如果動詞是 to be ，頻率副詞要放在 to be 後面。

主語	to be	動詞	句子其他部分
I	am	never	late for school.

頻率副詞放在 to be 後面。

更多例子

We **always** walk the dog in the evening.

Tom **usually** plays baseball on Tuesdays.

They **often** go on holiday to France.

We **sometimes** have pizza for dinner.

He is **never** bored at the park.

71 Intensifiers 強調詞

參見：
形容詞　第 63 單元
情態副詞　第 66 單元

The grey dog is dirty.
The brown dog is very dirty.

71.1「very」和「really」

在形容詞或副詞前面使用「very」或「really」。

主語	動詞	very或really	形容詞
The brown dog	is	very / really	dirty.

在形容詞或副詞前面加 very 或 really 。

主語	動詞	very或really	副詞
The brown dog	walks	very / really	slowly.

用法

用 very 或 really 加強形容詞或副詞的語氣。它們的意思相同，但 really 更口語化。

更多例子

The road is **very** busy.

Maria's dad is **really** tall.

Sofia can run **really** fast.

The grey dog is much bigger than the black dog.

71.2 「much」

在比較級形容詞或比較級副詞前面使用 much。

用法

用 much 加強比較級形容詞或副詞的語氣。

subject	verb	much	comparative adjective
The grey dog	is	much	bigger.

將 much 放在比較級形容詞前面。

subject	verb	much	comparative adverb
The grey dog	barks	much	more loudly.

將 much 放在比較級副詞前面。

更多例子

The rabbit runs **much** more quickly than the tortoise.

It's **much** colder in winter than in summer.

The drums are **much** noisier than the guitar.

72 Prepositions of place
位置介詞

參見：
動向介詞　第 73 單元
時間介詞　第 74 單元

72.1 位置介詞的用法

用位置介詞談論事物或人物的位置。

The cat is
in the box.

The cat is
on the box.

The cat is
next to the box.

The cat is
in front of the box.

The cat is
behind the box.

The cat is
opposite the box

The cat is
between the boxes.

The cat is
under the plant.

The cat is
below the tree.

The bird is
above the cat.

73 Prepositions of movement

動向介詞

參見：
位置介詞 第 72 單元
時間介詞 第 74 單元

73.1 動向介詞的用法

用表示動向的介詞談論事物或人物如何從一個地方移動到另一個地方。

The cat is walking **up** the stairs.

The cat is walking **down** the stairs.

The cat is jumping **into** the box.

The cat is jumping **out of** the box.

The cat is jumping **over** the box.

The cat is walking **under** the desk.

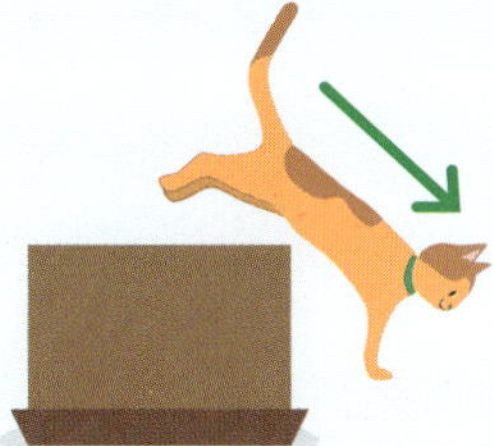

The cat is jumping **off** the box.

The cat is walking **through** the box.

The cat is walking **across** the garden.

74 Prepositions of time 時間介詞

用時間介詞談論事情發生的時間。

74.1「on」

用法

在星期幾或日期前面使用 on 表示事情發生、發生過或將要發生的時間。

74.2「at」

用法

在時間點前面使用 at 表示事情發生、發生過或將要發生的時間。

74.3「in」

用法

在月份、年份、季節和早上、下午和晚上這些詞前面使用 in 表示事情發生、發生過或將要發生的時間。

參見：
時間副詞 第 69 單元
時間詞 第 R28 單元

74.4「until」

You can play until dinner.

用法

將 until 與時間、日期、年份或事件連用，談論持續的動作或情況何時會結束。

現在

直到

他們打算在晚飯前停止玩耍。

74.5「from… to…」

We go to gymnastics from 10 o'clock to 1 o'clock.

用法

將 from…to…與時間連用，談論事情的開始和結束時間。

從

到

活動在 10 點鐘開始。

活動在 1 點鐘結束。

74.6「for」

用法

在表示一段時間的短語前使用 for，談論事情發生的時長。

兩個小時

他們在 4 點開始下國際象棋。

他們在 6 點結束了下國際象棋。

74.7「since」

用法

用 since 談論持續的動作或情況開始的時間。since 要與現在完成式連用，不能與簡單現在式連用。

自從

現在

活動在 11 點開始，目前仍在進行中。

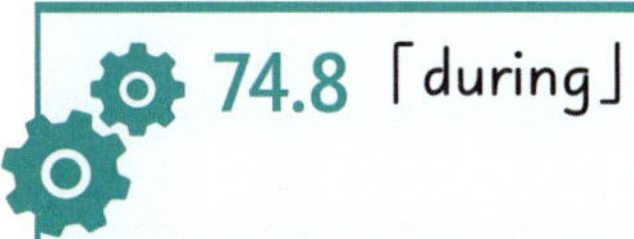

74.8「during」

用法

用 during 談論事情發生的時間段。

I went to the library during my lunch break.

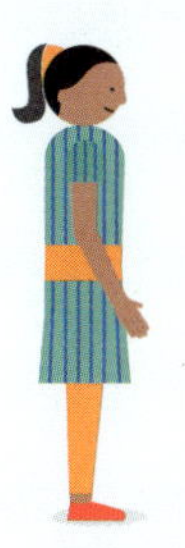

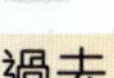

過去　在午休期間　現在

Sara 在午休期間的某個時候在圖書館。

74.9「by」

用法

在時間前面使用 by 表示事情將在該時間之前完成或結束。

I have to be home by 6 o'clock.

現在　在六點鐘之前

Max 必須在現在到 6 點之間到家。

74.10「before」

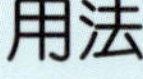

用 before 談論比其他事情更早發生的事情。

We usually walk the dog before dinner.

晚餐

這代表他們先遛狗，然後吃晚餐。

74.11「after」

用法

用 after 談論發生其他事情之後的事情。

I often read comic books after dinner.

晚餐

晚餐後

這代表 Max 先吃晚飯，然後看漫畫書。

更多例子

on	用於具體某天或日期，表示事情發生的時間。	I go to science club **on** Wednesdays. We played badminton **on** Friday.
at	用於具體時刻，表示事情發生的時間。	We eat breakfast **at** 7 o'clock. I catch the bus **at** 8 o'clock.
in	與某些時間詞連用，表示事情發生的時間。	I was born **in** the summer. My school has a party every year **in** July.
until	與時間詞連用，表示事情將結束的時間。	I have basketball practice **until** 4 o'clock. We have to stay here **until** we've finished.
from… to…	與時間連用，表示事情的開始和結束時間。	My Dad works **from** 9 o'clock **to** 5 o'clock. Lunchtime is **from** 12 o'clock **to** 1 o'clock.
since	用於談論某個持續動作或狀態的開始時間，常與現在完成式連用。	I've been here **since** 3 o'clock. We've been in Spain **since** last week.
for	用於談論事情持續的時長。	I have been at school **for** three hours. We played **for** two hours yesterday.
during	用於談論事情發生的時間段。	We played all day **during** the summer. Andy learned a lot **during** the lesson.
by	表示事情將在某個時間點之前完成或結束。	I have to finish my homework **by** 6 o'clock. We've usually eaten dinner **by** 7 o'clock.
before	用於談論先發生的事情。	I eat breakfast **before** school. Sara has football practice **before** dinner.
after	用於談論後面發生的事情。	We're going to the park **after** school. **After** breakfast, I catch the bus.

75 「With」和「without」

With 和 without 都是介詞，用在名詞前面。

75.1 「with」

Max came **with** me to the park.

用法

用 with 談論與其他事物同時存在的事物。

We stayed in a hotel **with** a swimming pool.

用 with 談論所屬關係。

Dad cut the apple **with** a knife.

用 with 談論用於執行動作的事物。

75.2 「without」

I had an ice cream **without** sauce.

用法

用 without 談論缺少事物的情況。

更多例子

Do you want to come to the cinema **with** us?

I'm going to buy a new toy **with** my money.

Mum made pasta **with** meatballs.

I like books **with** lots of pictures.

We drew our pictures **with** pencils.

They live in a house **with** a garden.

My dad likes tea **without** sugar.

Sara went to school **without** her books.

I prefer burgers **without** cheese.

76 Conjunctions 連接詞

參見：
分句 第 R6 小節

連接詞將單詞、短語、分句或句子連接在一起。

76.1 「and」

I like cars. I like rockets.

I like cars **and** rockets.

用 and 將兩個句子連接起來。

用法

用 and 談論不止一件事，或將談論同一事物的兩個句子連接起來。

76.2 「but」

I like apples. I don't like pears.

I like apples, **but** I don't like pears.

用 but 對比肯定陳述與否定陳述。

用法

用 but 將肯定陳述與否定陳述對比。

76.3「or」

I don't like dolls. I don't like cars.

I don't like dolls **or** cars.

用 or 連接兩個否定句。

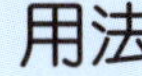

用法

用 or 將兩個否定陳述連接在句子中。

Would you like pasta? Would you like pizza?

Would you like pasta **or** pizza?

這代表在義大利面和披薩之間作出選擇。

當在兩個或多個事物之間有選擇時，使用 or。

76.4「than」

主語 + 動詞	比較級	than	句子其他部分
Your doll is	smaller	**than**	mine.

這是一個比較級形容詞。

在比較級形容詞或副詞後面使用 than。

用法

用 than 比較兩個或多個事物，用在比較級形容詞或副詞後面。前往第 64 和 67 單元，了解更多關於比較級形容詞和副詞的內容。

76.5「when」

這在第一個動作之後立即發生了。

甚麼時候	第一個動作	第二個動作
When	we got to the beach,	we went swimming.

這個動作先發生了。

用法

當談論兩件同時發生或緊接着發生的事情時，使用 when。

甚麼時候	進行中的動作	打斷性動作
When	I was playing tennis,	I hurt my knee.

正在進行的動作使用過去進行式。

打斷性動作使用簡單過去式。

當談論一個動作在另一個動作進行期間發生時，使用 when。

甚麼時候	第一個未來事件	第二個未來事件
When	I get home,	I'll do my homework.

這個分句雖然表示將來發生的動作，但使用簡單現在式。

你也可以在這些句子的中間使用 when 。

I'll do my homework **when** I get home.

當 when 位於句子中間時，不用逗號。

用 when 談論事情發生後，將會發生甚麼事情。

76.6「after」

你可以在句子開頭或句子中間使用 after。

這個動作先發生。

這個動作第二個發生。

I brush my teeth **after** I get up.

當 after 出現在句子中間時，不需要使用逗號。

用法

用 after 談論發生在其他動作之後的事情。

76.7「before」

你可以在句子開頭或句子中間使用 before。

這個動作第二個發生。

這個動作先發生。

I always read a book **before** I go to sleep.

當 before 位於句子中間時，不用逗號。

用法

用 before 談論比另一個動作發生得更早的事情。

76.8「if」

你可以在句子開首或句子中間使用 if。

如果	動作/情況	結果
If	I score a goal,	we'll win the game.

這是尚未發生的動作。

這將作為該動作的結果而發生。

We'll win the game
if I score a goal.

當 if 位於句子中間時，不用逗號。

用法

在條件句中使用 if，若想了解更多關於條件句中 if 的用法，可前往第 36 和 37 單元學習。

76.9「because」

動作	因為	結果
I've come to the vet	because	my cat is ill.

這是動作。

用 because 將一個動作和它的原因連接起來。

用法

用 because 說明事情發生的原因或解釋作出的決定。

76.10「so」

這是該情況導致的結果。

動作/情況	所以	結果
It's sunny today,	so	we've come to the beach.

這是情況。

用法

用 so 談論由於其他事情而發生的事情。

更多例子

and	連接談論同一事物的兩個句子。	Maria is wearing a red dress **and** blue shoes. I bought Ben a new toy **and** he loved it!
but	用肯定陳述與否定陳述形成對比。	I love swimming, **but** I don't like running. She can't sing, **but** she can play the piano.
or	用於否定句中表示兩個或多個事物，或表示事物之間的選擇。	I've never been to Spain **or** Italy. Do you want to play baseball **or** basketball?
than	用於比較級形容詞或副詞後面。	My dog is bigger **than** my cat. Max can run faster **than** Andy.
when	表示事情發生的時間。	**When** she got home, she practised the violin. I'll swim in the sea **when** I go on holiday.
after	描述比另一個動作發生得晚的動作。	Sofia went to bed **after** she ate her dinner. **After** I ran the race, I had a glass of water.
before	描述比另一個動作發生得早的動作。	I put on my pyjamas **before** I went to bed. **Before** Maria went outside, she put on a coat.
if	用於條件句中。	Don't go to school **if** you're feeling ill. **If** you tidy your room, we'll go to the park.
because	說明事情發生的原因或解釋某個決定。	I love reading **because** it's fun. We didn't walk to school **because** it's raining.
so	用於談論由於其他事情而發生的事情。	I was hungry, **so** I made a sandwich. Sara was tired, **so** she went to bed early.

Reference 參考

R1 英語字母表

英語字母表有 26 個字母，其中包含 5 個母音（vowels）：a、e、i、o 和 u，其他 21 個字母稱為子音（consonants）。

句子的首字母、人名、地名、星期和月份需用大寫字母（capital letter）。

其他情況下使用小寫字母（lowercase letters）。

Aa Bb Cc Dd Ee Ff Gg Hh Ii

Jj Kk Ll Mm Nn Oo Pp Qq Rr

Ss Tt Uu Vv Ww Xx Yy Zz

R2 標點符號

英語使用各種標點符號使句子更清晰。

標點符號	用法	例子
full stop 句號	在句子最後使用。	Maria likes oranges.
comma 逗號	連接兩個主句或分隔列表中的單詞。	I like pizza, but I don't like pasta. I love cars, trains, and rockets!
question mark 問號	在疑問句最後使用。	Do you like robots?
exclamation mark 感嘆號	在表達興奮等情感的句子最後使用。	Let's play football!
apostrophe 撇號	表示所屬關係或在縮寫中代替省略的字母。	Ben's cat is black. She's my sister.

R3 詞性

構成句子的不同類型的詞被稱為詞性。

詞性	定義	示例
noun 名詞	表示人、地點或事物的詞。	cat, Sara, girl, house, water
adjective 形容詞	描述名詞或代詞的詞。	big, funny, light, red, young
verb 動詞	表示動作或狀態的詞。	be, go, read, speak, think, want
adverb 副詞	描述動詞、形容詞或其他副詞的詞。	always, easily, happily, here, loudly, much, soon, very
pronoun 代詞	代替名詞的詞。	he, she, you, we, them, it
preposition 介詞	描述事物所在的位置、去向、時間，或引出一個對象或概念。	about, above, from, in
conjunction 連接詞	連接單詞、短語或分句的詞。	and, because, but
article 冠詞	置於名詞前面，表示名詞是特指還是泛指的詞。	a, an, some, the
determiner 限定詞	置於名詞前面，指明所談論的特定事物的詞。	her, my, their, your

R4 音節

音節是單詞的一部分。單詞中的每個母音音素構成一個音節。母音音素是單詞中包含 a、e、i、o、u（有時包括 y）的發音部分。

R5 句子的組成部分

所有句子都有一個動詞，而且大部分至少還有一個主語。句子可以包括直接賓語。

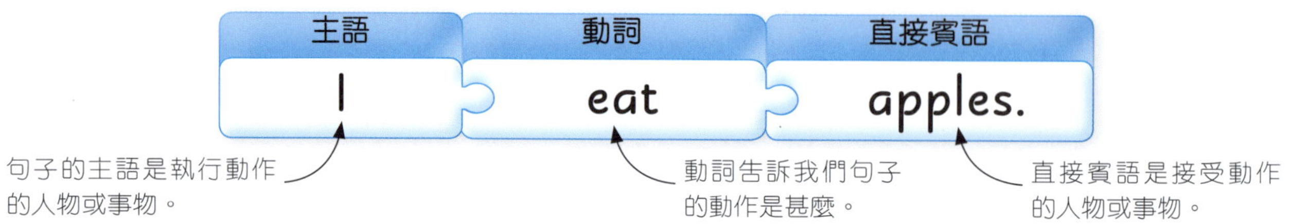

句子也可以包含間接賓語。一個句子要有間接賓語，就必須同時有直接賓語。

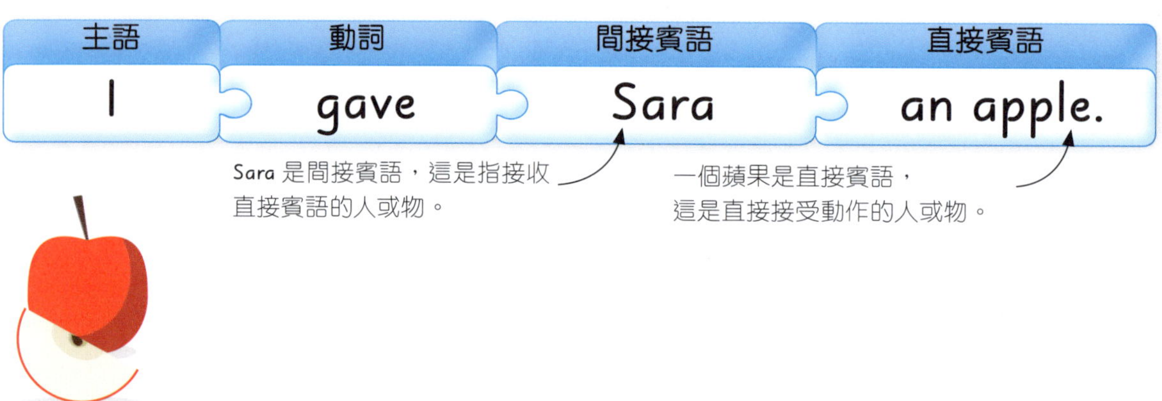

R6 分句

分句是包含主語和動詞的短語。有些句子包含兩個或多個分句。分句可以用連接詞和關係代詞連接在一起。

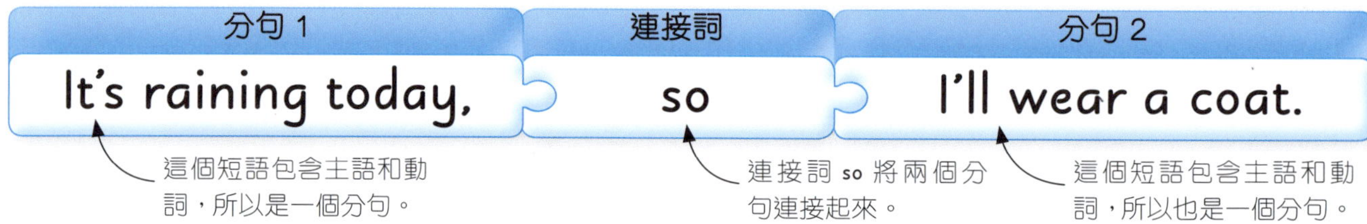

R7 規則動詞的簡單現在式

簡單現在式用於談論事實、觀點或經常發生的事情。規則動詞在簡單現在式中都遵循相同的模式。更多內容請參閱第 1 單元。

肯定句	否定句	疑問句
I like	I don't like	Do I like…?
You like	You don't like	Do you like…?
He likes	He doesn't like	Does he like…?
She likes	She doesn't like	Does she like…?
It likes	It doesn't like	Does it like…?
We like	We don't like	Do we like…?
You like	You don't like	Do you like…?
They like	They don't like	Do they like…?

R8 「To be」的簡單現在式

To be 是簡單現在式中的不規則動詞，不遵循通常的規則。to be 的簡單現在式用於談論事實、感受、情況和狀態。更多內容請參閱第 1 單元。

肯定句	否定句	疑問句
I am / I'm	I'm not	Am I…?
You are / You're	You're not / You aren't	Are you…?
He is / He's	He's not / He isn't	Is he…?
She is / She's	She's not / She isn't	Is she…?
It is / It's	It's not / It isn't	Is it…?
We are / We're	We're not / We aren't	Are we…?
You are / You're	You're not / You aren't	Are you…?
They are / They're	They're not / They aren't	Are they…?

R9 「to have got」簡單現在式

To have got 是簡單現在式中的不規則動詞，不遵循通常的規則。 To have got 簡單現在式用於談論所有權。更多內容請參閱第 1 單元。

肯定句	否定句	疑問句
I have got / I've got	I haven't got	Have I got...?
You have got / You've got	You haven't got	Have you got...?
He has got / He's got	He hasn't got	Has he got...?
She has got / She's got	She hasn't got	Has she got...?
It has got / It's got	It hasn't got	Has it got...?
We have got / We've got	We haven't got	Have we got...?
You have got / You've got	You haven't got	Have you got...?
They have got / They've got	They haven't got	Have they got...?

R10 現在進行式

現在進行式用於談論當前正在發生的動作。更多內容請參閱第 4 單元。

肯定句	否定句	疑問句
I am walking / I'm walking	I'm not walking	Am I walking?
You are walking / You're walking	You're not walking / You aren't walking	Are you walking?
He is walking / He's walking	He's not walking / He isn't walking	Is he walking?
She is walking / She's walking	She's not walking / She isn't walking	Is she walking?
It is walking / It's walking	It's not walking / It isn't walking	Is it walking?
We are walking / We're walking	We're not walking / We aren't walking	Are we walking?
You are walking / You're walking	You're not walking / You aren't walking	Are you walking?
They are walking / They're walking	They're not walking / They aren't walking	Are they walking?

R11 規則動詞的簡單過去式

簡單過去式用於談論在過去某個固定時刻完成的動作。更多內容請參閱第 8 單元。不規則動詞的簡單過去式列表，請參閱 R19 。

肯定句	否定句	疑問句
I played	I didn't play	Did I play...?
You played	You didn't play	Did you play...?
He played	He didn't play	Did he play...?
She played	She didn't play	Did she play...?
It played	It didn't play	Did it play...?
We played	We didn't play	Did we play...?
You played	You didn't play	Did you play...?
They played	They didn't play	Did they play...?

R12 「To be」的簡單過去式

To be 是簡單過去式中的不規則動詞，不遵循通常的規則。 To be 的簡單過去式用於談論事實、感受、情況和狀態。更多內容請參閱第 8 單元。

肯定句	否定句	疑問句
I was	I wasn't	Was I...?
You were	You weren't	Were you...?
He was	He wasn't	Was he...?
She was	She wasn't	Was she...?
It was	It wasn't	Was it...?
We were	We weren't	Were we...?
You were	You weren't	Were you...?
They were	They weren't	Were they...?

R13 過去進行式

過去進行式用於談論過去正在進行的動作或講故事。
更多內容請參閱第 11 單元。

肯定句	否定句	疑問句
I was running	I wasn't running	Was I running?
You were running	You weren't running	Were you running?
He was running	He wasn't running	Was he running?
She was running	She wasn't running	Was she running?
It was running	It wasn't running	Was it running?
We were running	We weren't running	Were we running?
You were running	You weren't running	Were you running?
They were running	They weren't running	Were they running?

R14 現在完成式

現在完成式用於談論最近的過去。更多內容請參閱第 14 單元。不規則過去分詞列表，請參閱 R19 。

肯定句	否定句	疑問句
I have arrived	I haven't arrived	Have I arrived?
You have arrived	You haven't arrived	Have you arrived?
He has arrived	He hasn't arrived	Has he arrived?
She has arrived	She hasn't arrived	Has she arrived?
It has arrived	It hasn't arrived	Has it arrived?
We have arrived	We haven't arrived	Have we arrived?
You have arrived	You haven't arrived	Have you arrived?
They have arrived	They haven't arrived	Have they arrived?

R15「Going to」

Going to 與動詞基本形式連用，用於根據證據做出預測或談論未來計劃。
更多內容請參閱第 18 單元。

肯定句	否定句	疑問句
I'm going to swim	I'm not going to swim	Am I going to swim?
You're going to…	You're not going to… / You aren't going to…	Are you going to…?
He's going to…	He's not going to… / He isn't going to…	Is he going to…?
She's going to…	She's not going to… / She isn't going to…	Is she going to…?
It's going to…	It's not going to… / It isn't going to…	Is it going to…?
We're going to…	We're not going to… / We aren't going to…	Are we going to…?
You're going to…	You're not going to… / You aren't going to…	Are you going to…?
They're going to…	They're not going to… / They aren't going to…	Are they going to…?

R16「Will」

Will 與動詞基本形式連用，用於談論剛才做出的決定、做出承諾和在沒有證據的情況下做出預測，或主動提出做某事。更多內容請參閱第 21 單元。

肯定句	否定句	疑問句
I will play / I'll play	I will not play / I won't play	Will I play?
You will… / You'll…	You will not… / You won't…	Will you…?
He will… / He'll…	He will not… / He won't…	Will he…?
She will… / She'll…	She will not… / She won't…	Will she…?
It will… / It'll…	It will not… / It won't…	Will it…?
We will… / We'll…	We will not… / We won't…	Will we…?
You will… / You'll…	You will not… / You won't…	Will you…?
They will… / They'll…	They will not… / They won't…	Will they…?

R17 情態動詞

情態動詞對所有主語都保持不變，he 、 she 或 it 後面不加 s 。它們後面通常接另一個動詞的基本形式。用 may 、 might 和 must 構成的疑問句很少見。 may not 沒有縮寫形式。更多內容請參閱第 28 單元。

肯定句	否定句	疑問句
can	cannot / can't	Can I...?
could	could not / couldn't	Could I...?
may	may not	
might	might not / mightn't	
must	must not / mustn't	
should	should not / shouldn't	Should I...?

R18 疑問詞

疑問詞用於問題的開頭。更多內容請參閱第 40 單元。

疑問詞	示例問題	示例回答
How 怎樣	**How** old are you?	I am nine years old.
How many 多少（用於可數名詞）	**How many** ducks are there?	There are five.
How much 多少（用於不可數名詞）	**How much** flour have we got?	We have got 1 kilogram.
What 甚麼	**What** is that?	It's a crocodile.
When 甚麼時候	**When** do you play badminton?	I play badminton on Saturdays.
Where 哪裏	**Where** is the cat?	It is under the table.
Which 哪個	**Which** dog is yours?	Rex is my dog.
Who 誰	**Who** is that?	It is Ben.
Whose 誰的	**Whose** camera is this?	It is mine.
Why 為甚麼	**Why** do you like football?	It is fun!

R19 不規則動詞

英語中有些動詞的簡單過去式和過去分詞形式是不規則變化的。以下是一些最常見的不規則動詞。

基本形式	簡單過去式	過去分詞
be	was / were	been
break	broke	broken
catch	caught	caught
choose	chose	chosen
come	came	come
do	did	done
draw	drew	drawn
drink	drank	drunk
eat	ate	eaten
find	found	found
forget	forgot	forgotten
get	got	got
give	gave	given
go	went	gone
have	had	had
hold	held	held
know	knew	known
learn	learned	learned
lose	lost	lost
make	made	made
put	put	put
read	read	read
run	ran	run
say	said	said
see	saw	seen
sleep	slept	slept
swim	swam	swum
tell	told	told
wear	wore	worn
write	wrote	written

R20 縮略式

我們經常會縮短一些動詞，尤其是在說話的時候。
以下是英語中最常見的一些縮寫形式。

代詞	to be	to have
I	I am ➔ I'm	I have ➔ I've
he	he is ➔ he's	he has ➔ he's
she	she is ➔ she's	she has ➔ she's
it	it is ➔ it's	it has ➔ it's
we	we are ➔ we're	we have ➔ we've
you	you are ➔ you're	you have ➔ you've
they	they are ➔ they're	they have ➔ they've
that	that is ➔ that's	that has ➔ that's
who	who is ➔ who's	who has ➔ who's

代詞	will	would
I	I will ➔ I'll	I would ➔ I'd
he	he will ➔ he'll	he would ➔ he'd
she	she will ➔ she'll	she would ➔ she'd
it	it will ➔ it'll	it would ➔ it'd
we	we will ➔ we'll	we would ➔ we'd
you	you will ➔ you'll	you would ➔ you'd
they	they will ➔ they'll	they would ➔ they'd
that	that will ➔ that'll	that would ➔ that'd
who	who will ➔ who'll	who would ➔ who'd

R21 縮略式：動詞＋「not」

我們經常會在縮短動詞後面跟着 not，尤其是在交談的時候。很少用 mustn't 和 mightn't。

動詞 + not		
is not ➔ isn't	had not ➔ hadn't	cannot ➔ can't
are not ➔ aren't	will not ➔ won't	must not ➔ mustn't
was not ➔ wasn't	would not ➔ wouldn't	might not ➔ mightn't
were not ➔ weren't	do not ➔ don't	could not ➔ couldn't
have not ➔ haven't	does not ➔ doesn't	should not ➔ shouldn't
has not ➔ hasn't	did not ➔ didn't	

R22 代詞、所有格形容詞和所有格代詞

想了解更多關於主格代詞的內容，請參閱第 51 單元。想了解更多關於賓格代詞的內容，請參閱第 52 單元。想了解更多關於所有格形容詞的內容，請參閱第 55 單元。想了解更多關於所有格代詞的內容，請參閱第 56 單元。 It 沒有所有格代詞。

主格代詞	賓格代詞	所有格形容詞	所有格代詞
I	me	my	mine
you	you	your	yours
he	him	his	his
she	her	her	hers
it	it	its	
we	us	our	ours
you	you	your	yours
they	them	their	theirs

R23 拼寫規則：現在分詞和動名詞

動詞的現在分詞和動名詞形式總是相同的。構成方法是在動詞基本形式後面加 ing 。有時在加 ing 之前，動詞基本形式的拼寫會發生變化。

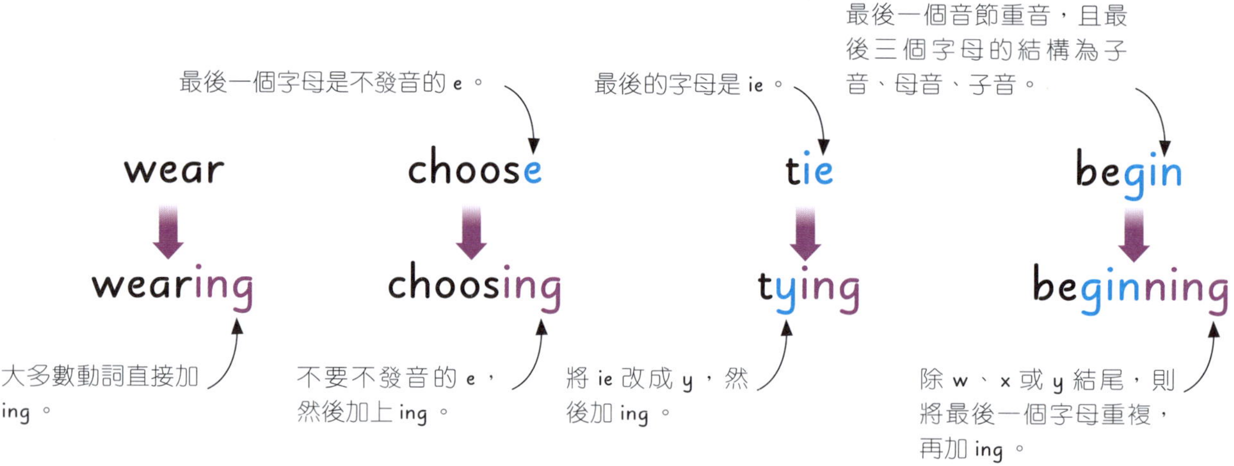

R24 拼寫規則：規則動詞的簡單過去式和過去分詞

對於規則動詞，它們的簡單過去式和過去分詞形式總是相同的。構成方法是在動詞基本形式後面加 ed 。有時在加 ed 之前，動詞基本形式的拼寫會發生變化。

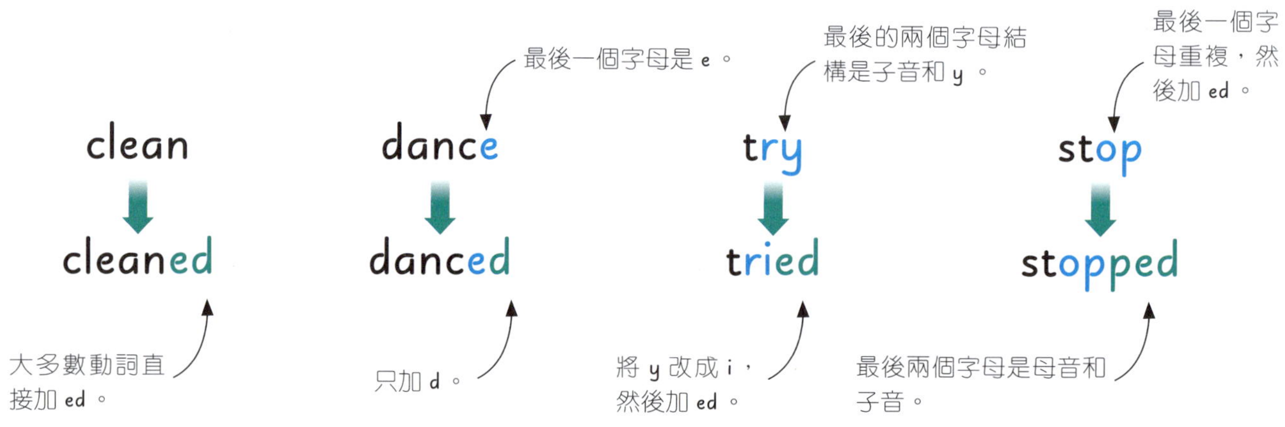

R25 拼寫規則：複數名詞

大多數名詞的複數形式是在單數名詞後面加 s 或 es 。

以 s 、 x 、 z 、 ch 或 sh 結尾的名詞加 es 。

大多數以 o 結尾的名詞加 es 。如果 o 前面有另一個母音，則直接加 s 。

以子音加 y 結尾的名詞，將 y 改成 i ，然後加 es 。

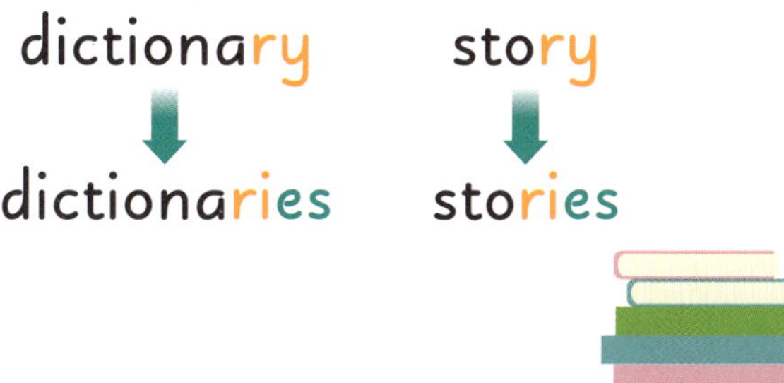

R26 不規則複數名詞

有些複數名詞是不規則的。它們變複數時拼寫方式會發生變化，或者完全不變。

單數	複數
mouse	mice
tooth	teeth
foot	feet
child	children
woman	women
man	men
person	people
sheep	sheep
fish	fish

R27 連接詞

用連接詞將單詞、短語或分句連接起來。

連接詞	用法	例子
after	用於談論在另一個動作之後發生的事情。	I get dressed **after** I eat breakfast.
and	用於談論多於一件事物，或連接兩個句子或分句。	I play the guitar **and** the piano.
because	用於說明事情發生的原因或解釋一個決定。	I'm wearing a jumper **because** it's cold.
before	用於談論在另一個動作之前發生的事情。	**Before** I have dinner, I wash my hands.
but	用於對比肯定和否定的陳述，或補充額外資訊。	I like robots, **but** I don't like trains.
if	用於條件句中，談論某個動作的結果或當事情發生時可能會發生的事情。	We'll go to the lake **if** it's sunny tomorrow.
or	用於談論兩個或多個事物，或在否定句中表示兩者之間的選擇。	I don't like pasta **or** rice. Would you like milk **or** juice?
so	用於談論事情因為另一事而發生。	I'm really tired, **so** I'll go to bed early.
than	用於比較兩個或多個事物，與比較級形容詞或副詞連用。	My cat is older **than** my dog.
when	用於談論兩件同時發生的事情，或事情在另一個動作進行期間發生。	**When** we got to the park, we flew our kites.

R28 時間詞

用時間詞談論事情發生的時間，它們可以是介詞、連接詞或副詞。

時間詞	用法	例子
about to	用於表示事情即將在很近的將來發生。	I'm **about to** eat dinner.
after	用於表示事情在另一事之後發生。	**After** school, I'm going to watch TV.
ago	與時間標記連用，表示事情發生至今已過去多久。	We got a dog a month **ago**.
already	用於表示事情已經發生。	School has **already** started.
always	用於表示事情總是發生。	I **always** wake up early.
at	用於時間前面，表示事情發生的具體時間。	School starts **at** 9 o'clock.
before	用於表示事情在另一事情之前發生。	We put our coats on **before** going outside.
by	用於表示事情將在某個時間前面完成。	I need to finish this **by** 6 o'clock.
during	用於表示事情發生的期間。	You shouldn't talk **during** class.
for	用於表示事情持續的時間長度。	I read **for** two hours today.
from... to...	與時間連用，表示事情的起止時間。	I played video games **from** 7 o'clock **to** 8 o'clock.
in	用於月份、年份、季節前面，表示事情發生的時間。	It's usually very cold **in** winter.
just	用於表示事情剛才發生。	I have **just** arrived home.
now	用於表示事情正在發生。	We're playing in the park **now**.
on	用於星期幾或日期前面，表示事情發生的具體日子。	We went to the lake **on** Saturday.
since	用於表示一個持續性動作的開始時間。	We've been playing **since** 4 o'clock.
soon	用於表示事情即將在不久的將來發生。	I'm going to go swimming **soon**.
still	用於表示一個從過去開始的持續性動作仍在進行。	We're **still** washing the car.
until	用於表示一個持續性動作將會結束的時間。	I'm going to draw **until** 5 o'clock.
yet	用於表示事情尚未發生。	I haven't got dressed **yet**.

Glossary 詞彙表

adjective 形容詞
A word that describes a ***noun*** or ***pronoun***, e.g. quick.

adverb 副詞
A word that describes a ***verb***, ***adjective***, or another adverb, e.g. quickly, very

adverb of frequency 頻率副詞
An adverb that tells you "how often", e.g. usually.

adverb of manner 情態副詞
An adverb that tells you "how", e.g. badly.

adverb of time 時間副詞
An adverb that tells you "when", e.g. soon.

apostrophe 撇號
The punctuation mark that shows either possession, e.g. John's cat, or a short form, e.g. I'm happy.

article 冠詞
The words a, an, some, and the, which show whether something is general or specific.
see also ***definite article***, ***indefinite article***

auxiliary verb 助動詞
A verb which is used with another verb, e.g. to form ***tenses***, most commonly to be, to do, and to have.
see also ***main verb***

base form 基本形式
The most basic form of a ***verb***, e.g. be, run, write.
see also ***infinitive***

cardinal number 基數
The numbers used for counting, e.g. one, two.
see also ***ordinal number***

clause 分句
A group of words that contains a ***verb***.

closed question 封閉式問題
A question that can be answered with "yes" or "no", e.g. Are you English?
see also ***open question***

comparative adjective 比較級形容詞
An adjective that compares one thing or group of things with another, e.g. taller.
see also ***superlative adjective***

compound tense 複合時態
A ***tense*** which uses an ***auxiliary verb***, e.g. the ***present perfect***: has done.

conditional 條件句
The verb structure used when one event or situation depends on another event or situation happening first.
see also ***first conditional***, ***zero conditional***

conjunction 連接詞
A word that links two words or groups of words, e.g. and, because, if.

consonant 子音
Most letters/sounds in English, but not a, e, i, o, u.

continuous 進行式
Continuous ***tenses*** express actions that are in progress at a specific time, e.g. I'm writing.
see also ***past continuous***, ***present continuous***

countable 可數的
A ***noun*** that can be counted, e.g. one book, two books.
see also ***uncountable***

definite article 定冠詞
The word the, which specifies the noun that follows it, e.g. the house in the woods.
see also ***indefinite article***

demonstrative determiner/pronoun 指示限定詞或代詞
Words that specify a ***noun*** as closer to (this, these) or more distant from (that, those) the speaker, e.g. This watch is cheaper than that one.

determiner 限定詞
A word that comes before a ***noun*** and identifies it, e.g. the book, this book.

direct object 直接賓語
The person or thing affected by the action of the ***verb***, e.g. "him" in We followed him.
see also ***indirect object***

first conditional 第一條件句
A sentence with "if" that describes a possible future situation that depends on another situation, e.g. If it rains, I'll stay here.

first person 第一人稱
When a pronoun or possessive adjective refers to the speaker, e.g. "I" in I am happy.
see also ***second person***, ***third person***

formal 正式用語
Formal language is used in situations where you don't know the people very well.
see also ***informal***

gerund 動名詞
The -ing form of a ***verb***, when it is used as a noun, e.g. No running.

imperative 祈使句
An order to someone, e.g. Stop! The imperative is a ***verb*** on its own in its ***base form***.

indefinite article 不定冠詞
The words a, an, and some which come before ***nouns*** to talk about something in general or for the first time, e.g. Can I borrow a pen?
see also ***definite article***

indefinite pronoun 不定代詞
A pronoun that does not refer to a specific person or thing, e.g. someone, nothing.

indirect object 間接賓語
The person or thing affected by the action of a ***transitive verb***, but is not the direct object, e.g. "the dog" in I gave the ball to the dog.
see also ***direct object***

infinitive (to-infinitive) 不定式（帶 to 不定式）
The ***base form*** of a ***verb***, with the infinitive marker "to", e.g. to go, to run.

informal 非正式用語
Informal language is used in situations where you know the people well and feel relaxed.
see also ***formal***

intensifier 強調詞
A word that makes an adjective or adverb stronger, e.g. very, really, and much.

intransitive verb 不及物動詞
A verb that does not take a ***direct object***.
see also ***transitive verb***

irregular 不規則
A word that behaves differently from most words like it, e.g. men is an irregular ***plural noun***.
see also ***regular***

main clause 主句
A ***clause*** that could form a complete ***sentence*** on its own.
see also ***subordinate clause***

main verb 主要動詞
The verb in a group of verbs that carries the meaning, e.g. "ride" in I can ride a bike.

modal verb 情態動詞
A type of ***auxiliary verb*** that is used with a ***main verb*** to show ideas like ability and permission.

negative 否定句
A ***sentence*** that contains a word like not or never.

noun 名詞
A word that refers to a person, place, or thing.

noun phrase 名詞片語
A ***noun***, ***pronoun***, or a number of words that are linked to a noun, e.g. the blue house.

object 賓語
A ***noun*** or ***pronoun*** that follows a ***verb*** or a ***preposition***.

object pronoun 賓格代詞
A pronoun that usually follows a ***verb*** or a ***preposition***, e.g. me, them.

open question 開放式問題
A question that cannot be answered with "yes" or "no". They start with a ***question word***.
see also ***closed question***

ordinal number 序數
The numbers used for ordering, e.g. first, second.
see also ***cardinal number***

participle 分詞
The form of a ***verb*** used to make ***compound tenses***.
see also ***past participle*** and ***present participle***

past continuous 過去進行式
A ***tense*** that is formed with was or were and the ***present participle***, e.g. was doing. It expresses an ongoing action in the past.

past participle 過去分詞
The ***participle*** form of a ***verb*** that is used to make ***perfect tenses***, e.g. walked, done, eaten.

past simple 簡單過去式
A ***tense*** that consists only of the past form of a ***verb***, e.g. walked, said, ate. It expresses a completed action in the past.

perfect 完成式
Perfect ***tenses*** express a link between two times, e.g. the ***present perfect*** links the past with the present.

person 人稱
The form of a ***pronoun*** that shows who is speaking (I, we), who is being spoken to (you), or who or what is being mentioned (he, she, it, they). ***Verbs*** also reflect person, e.g. am is the first person singular form of to be.

personal pronoun 人稱代詞
A word that refers to people or things that have already been mentioned, e.g. he, they.
see also ***object pronouns***, ***subject pronouns***

plural 複數
The form of a word used when there is more than one of something, e.g. books, they.
see also ***singular***

positive 肯定句
A ***sentence*** that expresses what someone or something is or does. It does not contain a negative word.
see also ***negative***

possessive adjective 所有格形容詞
A word that comes before a ***noun*** and shows possession, e.g. my, our, his.

possessive pronoun 所有格代詞
A word that replaces a ***noun*** and shows possession, e.g. mine, ours, his.

predicate 謂語
The part of a ***sentence*** containing a ***verb*** that describes what the ***subject*** of the ***sentence*** is doing, e.g. "likes apples" in Sara likes apples.

preposition 介詞
A short word that links two ***nouns*** or ***pronouns*** to show a relationship, e.g. to, at, with, from.

present continuous 現在進行式
A ***tense*** that is formed with the present of be and the ***present participle***, e.g. is doing. It expresses an ongoing action in the present.

present participle 現在分詞
The ***participle*** form of a ***verb*** that is used to make ***continuous tenses***, e.g. walking, doing.

present perfect 現在完成式
A ***tense*** that is formed with the present of to have and the ***past participle***, e.g. have done. It expresses an action that started in the past and is still continuing or that happened in the past but has a result in the present.

present simple 簡單現在式
A ***tense*** that consists only of the present form of a ***verb***, e.g. walk, say, eat. It expresses a general truth, an opinion, or a habit.

pronoun 代詞
A word that replaces a ***noun***, when the noun has already been mentioned, e.g. it, that.

proper noun 專有名詞
A noun that is the name of a person, places, days, and months, e.g. Maria, France, Sunday. Proper nouns always start with a capital letter.

question 問題
A ***sentence*** that asks for something, usually information.

question word 疑問詞
A word that is used to start some questions, e.g. what, which, who, why, how.

reflexive pronoun 反身代詞
A word that refers to the ***subject*** of the ***sentence***, when the subject and ***object*** are the same, e.g. myself.

regular 規則
A word that behaves in the same way as most words like it, e.g. books is a regular ***plural noun*** and waited is a regular ***past simple*** form.
see also ***irregular***

relative clause 關係分句
A clause that gives information about the ***subject*** or ***object*** of the ***main clause***.

relative pronoun 關係代詞
A word that introduces a ***relative clause***, e.g. who, that, which, where.

second person 第二人稱
When a pronoun or possessive adjective refers to someone the speaker is directly addressing, e.g. "You" in You are smiling.
see also ***first person***, ***third person***

sentence 句子
A group of one or more ***clauses***.

short answer 簡短回答
An answer to a ***question*** that only uses the ***subject*** and ***auxiliary verb***, e.g. Yes, I do.

short form 縮略式
Two words that are joined with an ***apostrophe*** to form one word, e.g. we are > we're.

simple tense 簡單式
Simple ***tenses*** are formed with a ***main verb*** only; they don't need an ***auxiliary verb*** in their ***positive*** forms.

singular 單數
The form of a word that is used to refer to just one person or thing, e.g. book.
see also ***plural***

statement 陳述句
A ***sentence*** that offers information, i.e. not a ***question*** or an ***imperative***.

stress 重音
Saying one ***syllable*** in a word, or one word in a ***sentence***, more strongly than the others.

subject 主語
The person, thing, place, etc. that usually comes before the ***verb*** in a ***sentence***.

subject pronoun 主格代詞
A word that replaces a ***noun*** as the subject of a ***sentence***, e.g. I, she, they.

subordinate clause 分句
A ***clause*** which is dependent on the ***main clause***, usually introduced by a ***conjunction***.

superlative adjective 最高級形容詞
An adjective that indicates the most extreme of a group of things, e.g. best.
see also ***comparative adjective***

syllable 音節
Every word is made up of a number of syllables, each of which contain a ***vowel*** sound, e.g. teach (one syllable), teacher (two syllables).

tag question 附加疑問句
A short phrase that makes a ***statement*** into a ***question***, e.g. "isn't it" in It's hot today, isn't it?

tense 第三人稱
The form of a ***verb*** that shows the time of the action, e.g. ***present simple***, ***past simple***.

third person 時間標誌詞
When a pronoun, name, or possessive adjective refers to someone who is not the speaker or is not being directly addressed by the speaker, e.g. "They" in They are playing football.
see also ***first person***, ***second person***

time marker 及物動詞
A word or phrase that indicates a time, e.g. now, yesterday, tomorrow.

transitive verb 及物動詞
A verb that takes a ***direct object***.
see also ***intransitive verb***

uncountable 不可數
A ***noun*** that cannot be counted, e.g. water, money.
see also ***countable***

verb 動詞
A word that refers to a situation or an action, e.g. stay, write.

vowel 母音
The English letters a, e, i, o, u.
see also ***consonant***

word class 詞類
Shows the function of a word in a sentence, e.g. ***noun***, ***verb***, ***adjective*** are all word classes.

word order 詞序
The position that different words have in a ***sentence***, e.g. the ***subject*** usually comes before the ***verb***.

zero conditional 零條件句
A ***sentence*** with "if" or "when" that describes a present situation or a regular action, e.g. When it rains, we stay inside.

Index 索引

所有數字均指單元編號。黑體標示的單元編號為主要內容，以 R 開頭的單元編號位於參考部分。

D

E

F

G

H

S

T

U

V

W

Y

Z

Acknowledgments 致謝

出版方特此致謝：

奧利弗・德雷克（Oliver Drake）進行校對，蘿拉・加德納（Laura Gardner）與傑西卡・塔波爾賽（Jessica Tapolcai）提供設計協助，以及伊麗莎白・懷斯（Elizabeth Wise）擔任索引編製。